THE
DARKNESS UNDER
the WATER

THE
DARKNESS UNDER
the WATER

· BETH KANELL ·

CANDLEWICK PRESS
CAMBRIDGE, MASSACHUSETTS

First edition 2008

Library of Congress Cataloging-in-Publication Data

Kanell, Beth
The Darkness under the water / Beth Kanell. — 1st ed.
p. cm.
Summary: In 1930, sixteen-year-old Molly lives under the shadow of a governor who wants to sterilize people "unfit to be true Vermonters," such as her
Abenaki family, while the loss of her family home, her mother's pregnancy, her
first love, and other events transform her life.
ISBN 978-0-7636-3719-4
[1. Coming of age — Fiction. 2. Family life — Vermont — Fiction.
3. Eugenics — Fiction. 4. Abenaki Indians — Fiction.
5. Indians of North America — Vermont — Fiction.
6. Vermont — History — 20th century — Fiction.]
I. Title.
PZ7.D8795Dar 2008
[Fic] — dc22   2007024969

2 4 6 8 10 9 7 5 3 1

Printed in the United States of America

This book was typeset in Sabon.

Candlewick Press
2067 Massachusetts Avenue
Cambridge, Massachusetts 02140

visit us at www.candlewick.com

For Nikia — *Oliwni*, thank you

• • •

SPRING

·✦·

There is nothing I like about April.

Here in Waterford, Vermont, at least the snow stops, and the days are bright, if they're sunny days. But mostly they are not sunny in April. They are gray, and cold, and I don't care how many daffodils my mother says are open in the garden or how many vases my grandmother fills with pussy willows cut from the scrubby bushes by the river.

Because the river itself fills all of April.

It rains for days here, hard enough to wash the soiled banks of snow away from the muddy roads. Everything smells like rain. Not the soft summer smell of damp fields, and not the hiss of rain that rides on thunderclouds. But wet, moldy, unforgiving rain that leaks through the roof, seeps under the doors, turns clothing musty and books soft and woolen coats endlessly damp and stinking of sheep.

Worst of all, when it rains all through April, the river thrashes and churns with froth and logs and power. It roars and crashes and I hear it all through the town—in school, at home, and especially all night in my bedroom, in the darkness. And I think about Gratia, who was my older sister that I never met. I think of her light brown curls, like the one in Mama's dresser drawer. I think about how she got up early on Easter morning sixteen years ago, in 1914. It was an April Easter, in a year when I wasn't born yet. But almost. Gratia got up all by herself that day and put on her new red shoes, and ran out in the rain to stand on the bridge and see the river. She loved to be the first one up, Mama once told me. When I was younger, I asked her often to tell me stories of the little girl so much like me. But now that I am fifteen, almost sixteen in fact, so much older than Gratia ever was, Mama's familiar stories leave me with questions.

What made Gratia go so close to the rail that day? There would still have been ice along the river edges. Maybe she tried to see into the flowing part of the river. Did she see something in the water, some log or drowned dog or someone's lost boat, lurching up and down, snagged and then torn loose again? Or maybe she dropped a stick into the water, like the village kids do still, and ran across the bridge to see it race out from the darkness underneath, in the rush of the southbound waters. Some days I imagine that her red shoes with their smooth new soles slipped on the wet wood of the bridge, slipped and slid with her under the railing. Other days I see her in my mind's eye, climbing the rail to lean over it and letting go by accident or by some bravery that I'll never have, daring to hang farther out over the waters.

One night I pictured her face as she fell—and it seemed I could almost hear her call out. To Mama? I would call for Mama if I were falling. But maybe it was Papa she screamed for.

And that, as anyone can see, begins a bad April night for me, a river-washed night of half dreams and fear.

But I don't wake Mama up ever. Lately she's cross so often, I wouldn't dare. I don't wake Papa, either, when he's there. I'm too old, and neither of them would understand, anyway. So I punch my pillow, turn it over to the cool side, lie in bed, and pray that Jesus, or maybe Gratia, will walk out of the dark corner of the room, glowing with a halo behind her soft curls. So soft and sweet and always the small child. And perhaps Mama would be happier, and Papa would stay home with us.

But that's imagination, and not truth. Papa says, "The truth will set you free." So last night, the nineteenth of April, the night before Easter, I climbed into the not-so-damp comfort of my bed, snuggling my feet against the hot water bottle that my grandmother provided. Outside, the rain rattled heavily on the windows and roof. I pulled the coverlet over my head to hush the sound, but I couldn't breathe enough, so I put my face back out into the chilly air after all, trying to decide what the truth of Gratia would be now. I suppose she would be married, have children, even. I would be an aunt. The thought gave me no pleasure, just a twist of the lip at the strangeness of time.

The wind rattled the window frame and hurled the scent of wet darkness into my bedroom. Easter was the resurrection of the dead, I knew; could Gratia come back to life? Not likely. Nobody I knew ever talked about our own dead being anything except guardian angels. Maybe she was an angel. With red shoes? Disgusted with my own imagining, I punched the pillow again and rolled over.

Accidentally I fell into sleep, into the dangerous current of dreams. Somewhere I stood at the rocky top edge of a cliff, voiceless and armless, shaking, alone—and last of all, there came walking out of a wet dark forest Gratia, my older but always five-year-old sister, dressed in something white and wet, dripping cold river water, standing beside me with white face and hands, saying something I wanted to hear but couldn't.

·✦·

I have a diary. It's bound in red leather with a miniature lock and key. Mostly I don't write in it while it's April.

But waking up just before seven on Easter morning, hearing Mama call sharply from downstairs and knowing it was the start of so much work and so little privacy for the day, I called down and said I'd be right there, then slipped the diary out of the bottom dresser drawer and wrote in pencil what was on my mind: "Easter Morning 1930. Sixteen years since Gratia drowned. Papa is not home yet from the woods. Four more days until my 16th birthday. Signed, Molly (Margaret) Ballou."

Like scratching a message on a cave wall on a desert island, nobody was going to see it, but I'd marked my being there.

A splash of cold water from the bowl on my nightstand pulled me further into the day, and although on any ordinary morning I would have squinted in the small pier glass at my reflection, checking for blemishes and trying to tighten the bodice around my chest more, today there was no time. I scrambled into wool stockings, linen shift, and my long navy skirt with a freshly pressed white blouse, and buttoned a lace collar at the neckline. The best part about long straight hair is that it combs quickly, and I slipped a blue ribbon around it to keep it out of my face. No braids today; it was a day for church, not school.

In the steamy kitchen, Mama dished up oatmeal into a bowl and pushed me toward the table. "The service starts at eight," she urged. "And you'll have to hurry home. I need you to set the tables."

"I know, I know," I said, trying not to let it sound like I was whining. Mama would lose her temper easily when she had so much to do. The aunts and uncles, and too many cousins, were coming from St. Albans for Easter dinner.

I looked over my shoulder toward the back bedroom as I poured maple syrup and cream over the oatmeal. My grandmother wasn't in the kitchen yet—or maybe, I thought sourly, she was out gathering more pussy willows for decoration. Or picking daffodils. I burned my mouth on the first spoonful but managed to speak anyway: "Where's Me-Mere?"

"Asleep." At my surprised look, my mother added, "She had a bad night. I'll wake her after you leave for church."

"Aren't you coming too?"

"And who'd watch the stove then?" Her voice rose, and I ducked my face. It wasn't like her to miss church on Easter Sunday, with the circuit minister offering services like we hadn't had for the past few years. But with Papa not home from the logging run yet, whether he was still in the woods or working the logs down the river, Mama had been moody and cross. I decided not to ask any more questions and just ate my breakfast as quickly as the steaming oats would allow. No "hot cross buns" for Easter breakfast, either, I observed.

Still, that was a small and ordinary change compared to the changes my aunts and uncles were bringing. But I didn't know that then. Breakfast and Sunday meeting clothes and deciding which almost-dry coat to spread across my shoulders for the run up the road to church were all I coped with.

Everyone says if a baby or little child dies, they've gone to be one of God's angels. So Gratia, you should be watching over me. But Gratia, if you're a guardian angel now, why didn't you stop things when they were simple?

Ah, well. No angels ever helped me before. I guess Easter shouldn't be an exception to what's true already.

I wiped my face, set my bowl and spoon into the metal dishpan, and ducked out of Mama's way, tugging on boots for the mud of the roadway. She pressed past me, apron flying, face flushed, thick and sturdy and strong, on the way to wake my grandmother. I glanced at the clock over the kitchen table: fifteen minutes until the church service. Four hours and fifteen minutes until company would arrive.

Catching some of Mama's urgency at last, I scurried out the door and away from the roar of the river, up the dirt road to the main street of the village. Everyone else in town seemed to be lined up to get into the white meetinghouse, while the rain poured over us. It leaked into my boots, giving me a cold and definite new something to think about, besides the hour and a half of prayer and hymns ahead of me.

I spotted my best friend from school, Katy O'Connor, and lifted a hand to wave. She smiled and called out to me but gestured toward her parents, and I understood: she needed to stay with them for the service. Well, since I had no family of my own to sit with this morning, I might as well join them. But what were they doing here, anyway? The O'Connors, who owned the general store at the other side of the bridge, usually drove the half hour to Littleton to worship at the Catholic church there. My grandparents had been Catholic before they came down from French Quebec, but my parents said it was more respectful to go to church in your own town. So I'd gone to Sunday school here and learned the Congregational ways. My father said it was a Vermont tradition anyway.

I edged through the double line and stood beside Katy, saying good morning to her parents and glad for the umbrellas they held over us all. The explanation for their being at the meetinghouse turned out to be simple: their car, famous in the village for its size and rumbling engine, was not working. Mr. O'Connor said something I didn't really understand, about a spark not being there, but what mattered to me was Katy being in church with me.

Mrs. O'Connor wore the sweetest, most lovely Easter bonnet I'd ever seen, and I told her so. Even in the gray morning, the pink silk roses on it glistened, and darker pink ribbons lay against her cheeks, to tie it in place. Katy's own bonnet, half the size but nearly as pretty, helped show off her creamy skin and red-blond curls. She gave me her famous crazy Irish grin when her mother stopped to talk with a neighbor, and whispered, "I've got to talk with you. Later!"

And although I sat beside her, my own soaked straw hat perched on my knee, the presence of her parents in the wooden pew meant we couldn't share any secret. Left to my inner conversation instead, I pictured Gratia coming back to life during each prayer, and also Mama being happy, and of course Papa, maybe even getting home this week. The bare white walls and polished woodwork didn't speak of angels to me, but of strength and firm words. No wonder I longed for Papa through the long worship service. Papa loved me even though Gratia was dead. Did Mama? Sometimes I wasn't sure.

If I were more of a good person, could Gratia be resurrected from the dead? If I prayed more? Not that I believed either of those was likely. Still, it gave me something to think about during the boring sermon that the Reverend Witherspoon gave. What would be better, Gratia next to me as a person again, or an angel? I closed my eyes as we all spoke the Lord's Prayer and tried to feel more grateful for my blessings. But it didn't work the way it used to when I was a child in Sunday school, where white-haired Mrs. Wheeler told us all that Jesus loved us and made it seem that Jesus could have been her own grown son, kind and warm and strong. That was for children, and I knew it. I tried to feel more holy, the way the hymn went, "Lord, I want to be more holy in my heart, in my heart." Mostly what I suddenly felt though was tired, tired of sitting in the thick, stuffy air of the church. My feet twitched in spite of me. I opened my eyes, and there was no angel next to the gold cross at the front of the church. Just in case, I squinted up toward the ceiling with my eyes squeezed so things blurred, but nothing sparkled or flew or sang in the air. *So what use is Easter?*

The swell of the organ in the final hymn let Katy lean close for just a moment and whisper, "In the school yard after dinner. If you can!"

I pressed her hand and nodded, and turned the page to the fourth verse of "Up from the Grave He Arose."

At least I had a best friend. Life could be worse. So with dinner for fifteen ahead, and Mama and

Me-Mere surely disagreeing with each other by now, I said a quiet "If I can" to Katy, ducked around the long line of people waiting to shake the minister's hand, and made my way through slightly gentler rain, to our wet, white house down by the river.

·✦·

Three roast chickens. Potatoes boiled and drained, ready to mash. Parsnips. Applesauce. Gingerbread and graham bread. Dried peach pie in the oven, and coffee, strong and hot, waiting.

Me-Mere sat in her rocking chair, watching down the road, hands moving automatically as she knitted something long and black in her lap. I hoped it was a sock, not a scarf, but I didn't dare to ask. The hours of dinner preparation exhausted all of us, with Mama pushing to make the meal, Me-Mere telling her what should have been done instead (dried apple pie instead of peach; a different way to roast the chickens; the other tablecloth because it had a longer hem; pick, pick, pick), and Mama finally snapping, "I married your son, not you!"

My own part, setting the table and opening jars of pickle and sauce, came easily enough. I would have dodged up to my room to stay out of the cross words, but every time I moved toward the stairs, one of them called me back.

Worst was the moment Me-Mere said to Mama, "You're not a true Daughter of the People, or you would respect me!" And Mama replied, "If you want respect, you have to be respectable!" Which for Mama was nearly as bad as using a cuss word, and shocked the three of us into silence for a long few minutes. Finally Me-Mere grumbled, "It's because you're expecting that you're so mean."

Expecting? I stared at Mama. Was she indeed expecting a baby? At her age? How could she?

But Mama's red face and hiss of anger confirmed what my grandmother had said, and I realized I hadn't questioned why she'd grown so thick in the waist. Yes, her skirts and apron disguised the swelling belly, but the minute the word *expecting* hit the air, I knew Me-Mere must be right.

"Mama?" I questioned her, so surprised that my hands stopped folding the napkins for the table.

"Not now," she said angrily. "And Mother, you're

wrong to talk about it before I've spoken with Charles."

Oh! I counted back to the end of December, when Papa had left for the woods. Four months. Five months to go. I started to say "September," but Mama cut me off with a sharp "Not now, I said!" and then with obvious reluctance added, "Your father knows, Molly. I wrote to him. But it's early, too soon to talk about it." One hand moved protectively to her waist. She glared at me and at my cross little grandmother, then abruptly burst into tears.

Enough: Me-Mere stood up and went over to Mama to apologize, and then Mama apologized to both of us — in words to her mother-in-law, and then to me, with a touch of her hand to the top of my head, stroking downward along my cheek. She said softly, "You're a good girl, Molly. And I know you'll be a help to me. But I don't want to talk about this yet. You understand, don't you?"

Because of Gratia. The shadow in our home, for me, and now for my mother. The missing child. I nodded and reached to hold her hand, but she pulled back, biting her lip, then patted my shoulder and turned toward the stove. I stood beside her a moment to help lift the heavy iron kettle of hot water.

And wondered: Boy or girl? And really, was it

safe to have babies so late in life? Mama was thirty-five years old!

Now I wanted desperately to talk with Katy, or at least to slip upstairs and write in my diary. But the clock showed a quarter to twelve, and the cousins and aunts and uncles would arrive in minutes. So with Me-Mere settled again in the rocking chair to keep watch, and Mama positioned at the stove with the gravy, I set out coffee cups and talked about Katy's mother's Easter bonnet and pretended it was all an ordinary holiday with just Papa missing, late from the winter woods.

Thinking of him focused me for a moment on the sound of the river again. Papa must be on the river by now, headed home to us. The wild brown river of power, collecting streams of winter melt and spring runoff as it wound its way down the eastern border of Vermont, toward the ocean two more states away. Though I hated and feared the river in spring, I knew it linked our town to the rest of the world.

The moment of thinking such geographic thoughts ended abruptly as a car pulled up outside the house, with a backfire of smoke and loud grinding of wheels and brakes. Me-Mere rose from her chair to reach the open door before my mother, calling out, "My sons! At last!" And Uncle Raymond and Uncle James and the aunts, Aunt Judith and Aunt Marie, with eight cousins scrambling to get out the big back doors of the car ahead of their parents, called out greetings and headed into our house, with news from beyond our town, news nobody wanted.

Like puppies.

The thought kept coming back to me as my aunts rounded up their boys again and again, to the table, from the table, into the kitchen to wash faces, into the parlor for games on the floor with tin soldiers and then a ball and jacks—all soon exiled to the back porch, along with the five boys. The three girls, Sarah and Josee and Anne Marie, carried dolls with them, and at my mother's urging, I led them upstairs to my bedroom, brought out my own old dolls, and let them all play, taking clothes on and off, braiding and tying ribbons on the long hair of each, talking and talking and talking.

Now even the girls seemed like round puppies, with giggles like baby dog barks. After a while, I almost believed they wagged their invisible tails in pleasure when I told them they were being good.

Almost sixteen, compared with Mama and Me-Mere, wasn't very old. But almost sixteen, compared to six, four, and three: I was a grown-up in this room of dolls and children.

Through the grating in the floor, where the warm air rose up to my room, I heard a change in the conversation down below. Edging closer, I lay on the braided wool rug and set my face close to the grating to listen. If I covered one ear to shut out the giggles of the girls, I could hear most of the conversation.

I didn't think they'd be talking about Mama's condition. Aunt Judith and Aunt Marie, sharp eyed and quick tongued, had teased Mama in the kitchen while we filled the plates, but in front of Uncle Raymond and Uncle James, "woman talk" usually vanished. No, they were talking about the governor. Politics. I started to roll back away from the grating, when Uncle Raymond's voice rose.

"It was in the newspaper, Caroline. Even here in this village you must read the newspapers. It's been in the newspapers for months now."

Mama said, "I don't have time to read the papers, Raymond. When Charles gets back, I'll catch up on news. Besides, I can't believe it's as bad as you say."

Uncle James's deep voice, quieter, replied: "It's bad. I think the French Canadians are worried, with the governor's commission saying they're breeding degenerates. But this Perkins fellow, he's already saying all our people are Gypsies, and at the statehouse, I read there's a bill being considered to sterilize anyone with Indian blood."

Silence fell downstairs. The little girls on the rug talked in the voices of the dolls, until even they seemed to notice something had changed, and they hesitated and looked over at me. "Why aren't you playing with us?" Josee asked me in her clear, high four-year-old voice.

I wriggled carefully away from the grating before turning to face her and the others and saying, "Let me fix the ribbons on that one."

I could almost sense the adults below, listening to us to see if we were listening to them, before the conversation picked up again. I strained to hear from my safer distance away from the grating, and heard one of the aunts ask, "Do people here in Waterford know about you? Did you ever say you're Abenaki?"

"French Canadian," my mother replied firmly. "Charles and me, that's what we are, what we've always said."

"Hrrmph." Uncle James, by the low sound. "French Canadian was good enough when it was only being Indian that we didn't want to say. But now, French Canadian sounds like trouble, too."

Back toward the grating I leaned, retying the ribbons on the doll's braids and smiling reassuringly at Josee, who began again to bounce two other dolls up and down, making them "talk" to one that Anne Marie was holding.

"Charles will know what to do," my mother declared. "And he'll be home in another few days, I'm sure of it."

The scrape of chairs and of the kitchen door opening told me one or two people chose the moment to step outside, and soon a whiff of cigar smoke confirmed that the men were smoking on the back porch, where the boys still played.

Of all of us cousins, no one else seemed to listen to the grown-ups and their worries. I suppose the others were all too young. I wasn't. I knew it wasn't polite to talk about having Indian blood, even if everyone guessed from my dark straight hair and shadowy skin that took the summer sun so easily. But more than being rude, was it dangerous now? Why? Did the governor hate us?

Without my noticing, my little grandmother must have climbed the stairs, for she stood in the doorway of my bedroom, watching us all. I met her gaze and knew she guessed I'd been listening.

I gathered three of the dolls into my lap over the protests of the little girls and began taking off the hair ribbons, to unfasten the Indian-style braids.

"Comb out their hair so it's pretty," I directed my cousins. From my rag-rug island in the middle of the wide board floor, I saw my grandmother nod in agreement and leave the doorway to return to the kitchen. Me-Mere and I would have to keep watch against danger. After all, Mama was expecting. And Papa wasn't home.

I wished so hard that it almost turned into a prayer: *Let Papa come home soon. Please.*

·✦·

Although I thought about Katy most of the afternoon, there was no chance to escape to the school yard to see her. I played big sister to the little-girl cousins while the aunts and uncles talked. Once, I went downstairs to the kitchen to help put away the dishes. But Mama sent me upstairs again, where I spread a blanket over a table, its edges reaching the floor, and helped Josee and Anne Marie play house inside it, while Sarah pretended to come visiting them. When the littlest ones seemed tired, I got out my copy of *Peter and Polly in Summer* and read to them about the boy and girl who lived just a few miles away, on a farm. Josee fell asleep at last, thumb in her mouth, and I showed the others the treasures in my jewelry box: my Chinese bracelet, and the pressed flowers Katy had given me, and my hair ribbons. They wanted to try the hair ribbons, so I combed their long, silky, dark hair and showed them ways to tie the ribbons.

"No braids on you today," I told them.

Finally, oh finally, the scrape of chair legs below and a rise in voices announced the end of the family visit. Aunt Marie came up to carry Josee. With Mama and Me-Mere, I stood at our front gate, watching the cousins settle into the backseat of the car with Aunt Marie, while Aunt Judith folded her skirts around her in the front seat, between Uncle James and Uncle Raymond.

Looking at their weathered faces and hands and the smooth dark hair of the women, the bristling thick hair of the men so quickly covered by their hats, I thought, *If it is dangerous now to be an Indian, what comes next?*

The three of us waved good-bye to the car full of relatives. Mama and Me-Mere said they wanted naps, and I said I had plenty to do. There was still some afternoon light; it was barely five o'clock. So after I set the kitchen table quietly for our supper, I changed from my Sunday skirt into my ordinary one, pulled on a hat and long rainproof mackinaw, and slipped out of the house at last.

Up the hill to the main street and over three buildings to the empty school yard I walked, not surprised that Katy wasn't there. Maybe she hadn't even been able to go there at all, but if she was there right after dinner, she must have been home again for hours now. Just in case, I went into the fenced school yard for a moment and looked in our secret place by the back gate, but there was no note for me.

The river sound rumbled endlessly, and a pair of crows sailed overhead. Their dark calls in the misty gray ending of the afternoon gave me no comfort. I hate April, every bit of it.

Moving away from the river, I walked slowly along a farm lane that headed from the village toward Fairbanks Hill. Only a few scattered houses interrupted the fields here; an occasional window glowed with early lamplight, but I saw no one outside. I scolded myself for thinking that anyone else would want to walk in the gloom of a late April afternoon, when they were full of Easter dinner and tired from the holiday.

And yet—there was one other person out walking after all. I saw him as I rounded the curve in the road, almost to the new cement bridge that crossed a thick, crashing, brown stream headed for the river. Short, with a pair of baskets hanging from a yoke on his shoulders, the boy hurried across the bridge. Twigs and sticks of willow stuck up from both baskets. The basket boy: Henry Laporte. I raised one hand partway, just enough to say "I see you," not enough to say "hello."

He nodded slightly, keeping his face mostly tilted down, barely meeting my eyes. I supposed he was embarrassed about working on Sunday, but Papa always said farmers had no choice. Maybe the basket boy didn't either. Maybe he had to get twigs for his family, for Monday's workday. Anyway, the load looked awkward—the sticks poked at his green and black wool jacket, and his hair hung limp and damp over his forehead. A mist curling up from the stream sent a tendril around his legs, and to my surprise, he stopped a few feet from me.

"Hey," I murmured.

I strained to hear the word he spoke. At the question in my face, he repeated it:

"Bear."

His shrug and a twitch of one hand pointed across the stream, up the road. I didn't see a bear. But I believed him, and nodded.

"I'll go back," I answered. "I don't have to go up there."

He nodded in return and starting walking again.

I walked a few feet from him, careful not to splash with my feet. The basket branches glistened with rain. Now I noticed the rain had stopped falling, although the mist moved with us, drifting along the bare fields. Gray light hung in the mist, and though I looked to both sides, to avoid staring at the basket boy, there was little else to see. I quickened my steps toward the village, and so did he.

"Won't hurt you," he said at last. "But you don't want to worry her, this time of year."

"Baby bears? Cubs?"

"Mmm," he agreed. "Someplace close."

I stole a glance at his face, thinking about the news I'd heard at home. Did his family say they were French Canadians, too? Seeing them bringing handmade baskets to the store and walking in the woods so much, well, anyone would know they were Indian, Abenaki, People of the Dawnland. The People. Curiosity pushed me to ask an indirect question: "When the rains end, will your family go to Canada?"

Startled, he tripped, caught himself, looked again at me, and said the most I'd ever heard from him. "Lunenburg, that's all, up past the long falls. We have a camp there. A cabin," he clarified. He looked away again, and added more: "My mother makes baskets, and gets the plants."

"Mmm. I know about the baskets."

"You do?" This time he stopped walking and turned toward me. "You make baskets too?"

"No. I don't make baskets. I mean, I know your mother does. Do you do it too?"

"No. Only my mother, and my sister. It's for women, that's all."

Oh. That must be how a traditional Abenaki family did things—baskets by women. Men in the woods. Well, how should I know all about Henry's life? I had barely spoken to him before. Even before he left school for work, he never came much. But I resented the suggestion that maybe I was ignorant, and I pushed back: "Well, you carry the sticks, don't you?"

"Mmm." His face cleared, and he walked again, a bit more slowly. "Did you ever learn to make them?" he asked.

I guessed he was trying to figure out my family too. Right about then, I wasn't sure how much to say. But I felt defensive.

"I don't want to make baskets," I answered honestly. "My grandmother can do it though, if she wants." To his nod, I added, "I go to school—and at home, I already do enough girl's work. I clean and I cook, and today I took care of children too. But I like

31

the woods." For a moment we both walked silently, and I watched his long, slim fingers resting on the baskets as his legs swung. His hands looked cool and quiet. Impulsively, I asked, "Is it hard to find the right sticks?"

He stopped walking, and we stood almost facing each other. He ran a finger gently along the length of one of the yellow-brown willow twigs. "Yes and no," he said at last. "It takes learning. But willow loves to bend, and if you put your hand on it, you can choose what feels right." Cocking his head sideways, looking quickly at me, then back to the twigs, he offered, "Maybe you'd like to learn that part. Maybe you want to ask my mother about it?"

"No!" Talk about basket willow with his mother, a person I didn't know at all? Not me. "No, thank you anyway. I was only wondering about the trees," I added politely. If Papa were home, he'd show me the willows in the woods. And if I were a boy, I could walk there by myself, just like Henry Laporte. Or if I knew more about these woods, I could maybe even show Papa! I wanted him home more than anything.

More words spilled out of me without thinking, too fast to stop them. "Would you show me where you go to get the willow branches?"

He shot another glance at me, hesitated, then said slowly, "No. Not the willow. I could show you the black ash on the mountain, some day. When it stops raining."

"I still have school for another week," I warned him. "I could go on Saturday maybe, if it's not raining then."

He nodded again, and suddenly pointed at a narrow dirt road across a cornfield, where the stubble poked up black and wet. It was almost dark. "My house is back that way," he finished. "Maybe Saturday, then."

Saturday. I'd have to ask Mama for permission. I want to walk in the woods to see some trees, that's what I'd tell her. With someone from The People, who can tell me things. She might be surprised, but she'd say yes, I was sure. Oh, dear, what if Henry thought I meant something, umm, something more like girl and boy together? I'd been so quick to ask him. I'd better make sure he understood too. So I tested this: As he turned off the road, I called out, "Mind if I bring my best friend, Katy?"

Without turning, he shrugged his shoulders, and I heard him call back, "It's a long walk."

"She can do it," I assured him. A shrug and a

small nod followed, as I watched him pick his way among the puddles and mud. I decided that meant Katy could come, and the prickle of uneasiness I'd suddenly felt at telling Mama I'd be walking on the mountain with this boy faded away. If Henry Laporte didn't mind my bringing a friend, it really was just to walk in the woods. So I wouldn't have to argue with Mama or Me-Mere, would I? I scolded myself for making a big deal out of it all. Why on earth had I talked with the basket boy anyway?

But I knew why: I missed Papa, and the dark, gentle face of Henry Laporte fit somehow into that missing, that loneliness. Also, I liked the quietness, the cool stillness that seemed to come from the basket boy even when he was answering a question. I'd been riding a river of people and hurrying all day. Standing in the road with Henry Laporte felt more like resting, more like a quiet kind of lake.

I decided to keep the moment to myself for now, and also the "maybe" Saturday walk. Mama was expecting, I reminded myself. She didn't need more to worry about. Not that this was anything to worry about, anyway. And Saturday was still a long ways off.

Still, by Saturday, it would be almost May. April, no matter how wet and long, would end. I edged around a wide muddy puddle and stepped back onto Water Street, glad to return to the heart of the village as the gloom around me deepened and the heavier rain pelted my mackinaw and my hot and sweating face.

·✦·

Gratia.

Though darkness hung silently over my bed, I knew she was there. In the corner. As I woke from the nightmare of people without faces and trees that tapped against the windows, I smelled river water and death. Someone must have the calendar wrong: Easter's gone, but Gratia's here now. That's what I thought. Or knew.

I drew in a thin, quiet breath, and the cool air confirmed I wasn't dreaming. In a dream I don't feel, taste, touch—I only hear, see, chase, dread. If cool air entered my nose, then this must be real. River water and death, said the scent in my face.

Frozen against the pillow, I waited. *When your drowned sister comes into your bedroom, does it mean you're about to die?* Every muscle clenched. At last I had to let out the breath I was holding, and when I started to inhale, I smelled it again. The river.

A crash downstairs tore at my tense legs. In spite of myself, I twitched and then grabbed at the blanket to pull it up against my face.

My grandmother whispered at the doorway: "Don't wake your mother. Come help me. Now."

The very real sounds pushed aside the sense of nightmare. The smell of river was still in my room. But if my grandmother told me to come, it couldn't be Gratia here, could it?

Another crash downstairs, a thump against the kitchen table, a scrap of light up the stairway. My sweater hung next to the bed. I eased out of the covers and pulled the sweater to me, the sweater my grandmother had made. "Gratia?" I hissed into the dark.

No answer.

Staying as far from the darkest corner of the room as I could, I edged out and crept down the stairs. The smell of river grew stronger. So did the sound of Me-Mere whispering. And someone else.

"Papa!" I choked out, and jumped down the last two stairs and into the kitchen to grab at him, colliding against his wet coat. His arms tightened around me, and I smelled not just river but my father's familiar mix of wood and bark and himself.

"That's my girl," he rumbled into the hair on top of my head. And in surprise, "My very tall girl!"

Me-Mere pushed at my shoulder, and I pulled back from my father just enough to see her smiling but also gesturing at me.

"Go back upstairs and get dry clothes for him," she urged in a low voice, and repeated, "Don't wake your mother!"

So it wasn't Gratia here in this night, was it? It was my father, in river-wet clothes. Relief flung me up the stairs, and then I tightened again into tiptoe and slinkiness, easing into Mama's and Papa's room, lifting an armful of his clothes from the closet hooks and slipping back down the stairs. Coat and shirt off, my father stood with his back to me, bending over the kitchen sink as Me-Mere poured warm water over his hair. Concentrating on keeping quiet, I spread out the clothes on a chair and pulled out a shirt and pair of pants. At Me-Mere's gesture, I turned around, my own back to Papa, so he could change into dry trousers.

"Coffee," Me-Mere ordered, and without peeking at Papa, I moved toward the stove and opened the damper, adding some kindling and urging the coals to redden and catch. There was coffee in the big blue and white pot from the night before; I slid it to one of the stove lids over the firebox and adjusted the damper again as the fire began to crackle.

From the sounds behind me, I tracked progress: My father finished washing, toweled off, pulled on dry clothes. My grandmother took the river- and rain-soaked ones out to the shed, and I turned back around to feast on the sight of my father, home from the winter woods.

He was thin, thinner than I remembered, and creases in his cheeks spoke of bone-deep tiredness. With his fingers he combed back his thick dark hair, grown out during the winter. Then he cracked a smile and awkwardly patted a long hand against my shoulder.

"You grew," he noted again, squinting at the height where I might have been before he left for the winter, then looking into my face. He was right— he wasn't taller than me now.

I grinned and replied, "Or the river water made you shrink. Like a frog in a winter burrow." As I realized what other kinds of growing I'd been doing,

I tugged at my sweater to make sure it was buttoned all the way. But thank goodness, it was; who needs to be teased in the middle of the night about things like that, anyway.

Me-Mere hushed us and herded us farther away from the open stairway. "Sit down at the table," she urged. "Quiet!"

Trying to whisper, I asked, "Was it a good winter? Did you get the logs down to McIndoe Falls already? Is everyone safe?"

"More or less," my father nodded. "One broken leg and one drowned horse. But the logs are still upriver. There's a jam near Lancaster. It'll blow later today, and I need to get back for the Falls."

Everyone in town wanted to see the logs go through the Fifteen Mile Falls. It would be the last time: The dam being built at Waterford would push the waters back into a lake, covering the rocks and rush of the long rough cascades. There would be no more river log drives after this spring, everyone said so.

I got up to pour hot coffee and noticed my grandmother beating batter for pancakes, so I carefully pulled out three plates and dug into the drawer for forks.

"Another plate, miss," said my mother's voice from the foot of the stairs. My father stood to embrace her, and I looked at the table instead of at them, fussing with napkins and cups. Too much emotion. My grandmother seemed to feel the same way, focused at the stove. Or maybe she just needed to check the pancakes as they sizzled.

After a long moment, I injected a question: "So there won't be school today, will there? Because everyone will be at the river?"

My mother agreed, now detached from my father's arms. Already she looked so much happier, and lighter, as if my father being home helped carry even the weight of the baby inside her. I liked the way she kept looking at him and smiling, and the way he smiled back at her. Now home felt right again. I pushed against her gently, and for the first time in just about forever, she rubbed my back and placed a kiss on top of my head. My home was mended at last.

I glanced outside and saw the light already increasing, and guessed, "Is it about five o'clock?" At my grandmother's nod, I said, "I'll get Katy at six."

"Wait until seven," advised my mother. So I sat down with them all and lingered over my own coffee and pancakes, listening to my father slowly answer my mother's questions about the long winter away. From the world of men and horses and trees, to the world of women: Did it feel strange to him? I wanted him to take charge again, to keep everything right. And safe.

A movement in the hallway caught my attention for a moment: it was my grandmother, reaching for the bundles of dried sage that hung from the rafters there. She beckoned to me to help, so I stepped next to her, stretched upward, and carefully removed the gray-green, prickly and fragrant bunches from the nails jutting out of the rafters.

"What are we doing?" I asked her.

"Brushing out the braids to make it look pretty." She echoed my words to the little cousins, with a half smile, a half wince.

Brushing out the braids? Oh. She meant our home and its Indian-ness under the surface.

I turned to look at my father, wondering when it would be time for my mother and grandmother to tell him the news about the governor, from the uncles and aunts. The creases in his cheeks, the tiredness in him under the effect of the coffee and food, the darkness of his skin from the winter sun on the snow: to me, everything about him said Abenaki, or Indian, one of the People.

To my grandmother's understanding nod, I said only, "He won't be easy to brush out and make pretty, will he?"

"It's not the first time," she replied. "We'll find ways. And he has his own too. Hand me that sack."

More curious now about my parents as Abenaki, I asked my grandmother, "Why doesn't Mama do the things you do? With plants, and the woods, and all? Didn't she grow up with the old ways, the way you raised my father?"

"She did," Me-Mere confirmed. "Up in Canada. But it was her time to change when she came south, and I told her I wouldn't push her, if she married my son." She added even more quietly, "She works hard."

I pressed for more of an answer: "Did you want someone who'd be more like you? To marry Papa?"

Firmly she said, "I wanted him to work hard and have a strong wife."

There was another question I wanted to ask, a question about Gratia. But not with Mama so close by. I helped my grandmother carry her baskets of dried leaves and stems, and we lifted them to back corners of the highest shelves in the porch beyond the kitchen.

·✦·

My father wasn't the only man from Waterford on the river; Katy's family knew the log drive would start coming through the Falls by afternoon if the men were lucky, or during the night if they weren't. For the O'Connors, the store would be busy all day and even longer. When I reached the store at seven, it was already open, a pair of trucks waited for the gas pump, and Katy, a long apron tied around her, was cutting huge slices of apple pie and gingerbread, getting ready for the crowd. I realized right away that she couldn't leave, so I asked for an apron and joined her while her mother ran the register and wrote up people's accounts. The scent of horse and cow drifted through the store, a pleasant backdrop to the men whose work clothes carried the aroma. Soon women began arriving, too, some to shop, some with picnics all made up in hampers, children under foot.

Mrs. Wheeler, from church, came without her husband, saying he'd be along later. She chatted with Mrs. O'Connor, and I overheard part of it.

"Jeannette, I was so pleased to have you worship with us on Easter Sunday," Mrs. Wheeler cooed, stroking Katy's mother's arm as she spoke. "You know, it's very American, the Union Meetinghouse for worship. I'm sure your Catholic ways were suited to Ireland, but here, things are different, you know. We can make real Yankees out of your family here. I'm sure it will be better for you, dear."

I peeked behind me and saw Mrs. O'Connor gently extract her arm and give Mrs. Wheeler's hand a squeeze. "Why, you know that Mr. O'Connor and I love this town," she said very clearly, maybe a little loudly. "We enjoy the chance to worship here with you, Mrs. Wheeler. There's nothing like an Easter morning service to bring out the best in all of us, don't you think?"

Sideways, I caught Katy's eye. Her golden necklace with the crucifix on it, the one her mother gave her for confirmation, dangled in front of her apron.

As we both listened, though, Katy tucked the little gold cross inside her blouse, out of sight.

Hmm. So Irish Catholic might be as much trouble as French Catholic, I considered. And both of them nearly as bad as Indian. Thank goodness I hadn't braided my hair, but maybe she could still tell. I supposed Mrs. Wheeler would head my way next. I turned and said to Katy, "Could you excuse me a minute?" And I slipped out back, into the storeroom, wondering whether I could stay there until Mrs. Wheeler left the shop.

In a few minutes, Katy appeared. She said, "It's safe, she's outside with the Fletchers." It should have been funny, but it wasn't. We stared at each other, and Katy held up the morning newspaper. "Look at the headline."

It read, "Governor Vows: Vermont for Real Yankees."

"Is that why your family came to Easter worship in the village yesterday?" I asked her.

"I suppose so."

Glumly, we looked at each other and at the newspaper. But a call from the storefront took us scurrying back to Katy's mother, to put groceries into boxes and fetch more bread for the wire racks.

I still didn't know what Katy had wanted to tell

me Sunday. At noon, Mrs. O'Connor sent us outside with sandwiches and apples for "a short breath of air," and I finally had a chance to ask.

She swallowed a large mouthful of bread and ham and told me, "I'm riding to town next Saturday with Jimmy Johnson. He's taking me to the afternoon movie matinée. And he said I could ask you to come too!"

"Yes!" Then I realized: "Oh, no. I mean, I want to go. But—I told Henry Laporte I'd go see where he finds the black ash trees for making baskets. And he said that I could ask *you* to come too!"

We laughed. Katy exclaimed, "First dates for both of us, the same day!"

"Except mine isn't a date," I told her. "It's just to see the trees. And walk in the woods with someone who knows something about it and won't get lost. But I'll tell him I can't go this Saturday," I assured Katy. "Going to the movie will be much better. And in all this rain, who could walk in the woods, anyway?"

So we agreed. *Besides,* said a small voice within me, *everyone in town is trying to seem like everyone else. I should too. So wouldn't it be dangerous to go walking with someone as obviously Indian as Henry Laporte, the basket boy?*

At that moment, shouts from the crowd by the

river told us that the logs must be coming into view. I said, "Let's go see!"

But Katy said, "My mother might need me. You go ahead, and when I can come, I'll meet you over at the bridge."

·✦·

I made my way among the neighbors crowded next to the river and stepped onto the covered bridge. About a dozen younger kids had the same idea, and they crouched at the gap where the trusses met at midriver, for the best view of the water. I moved close. Two other girls from the older grades stood hunched over the smaller children, and I joined them, asking whether they had seen any logs yet.

"Not yet," said Marion Simpson. She pointed toward the riverbank. "But there's Jimmy Johnson, and it looks like he's going into the water!"

Sure enough, there was Jimmy, the one who'd invited Katy, and also me, to the movie for next Saturday afternoon. He stood braced, with his boots straddling a muddy outcrop that the water rubbed against, with a peavey in his hand, a pike pole, to prod the logs away from the bank. Though there weren't any logs there yet, he leaned against a rock that jutted into the foam and noise of the river, the pole pressed against his shoulder, staring upstream. A little boy pressing toward the three-foot-wide gap of the bridge rails threw a stick into the water with a shout, and quickly I grabbed the child's jacket and said, "Stay back from the edge!"

Marion and I pulled all of the children back some and made them lie down instead of kneeling or standing. I looked over at our neighbors in the cluster on the riverbank to see whether the parents of the children would agree with what we'd done. Nobody looked up at the bridge. They were all focused on the river, staring upstream. The fog of the morning began to turn into steady rain, and though the bridge roof was some protection, I tucked my hair more firmly under my hat and rested one hand on a truss of the bridge. I looked down at the childen, then upriver at the crashing water, then down again.

Gratia.

I shook off the thought and focused resolutely on the children at my feet. All but one were boys; the girl, I saw, was a Larson, which didn't surprise me. She wore a pair of trousers, stained with barn and yard mud. Doubtless she'd borrowed them from a brother. I pursed my lips in scorn at such a boyish outfit on a girl in town, where she ought to dress better. Feeling my face scrunch up in disdain, though, I decided I didn't like that about myself, so I tried to cast off the scolding voice that sounded like my mother inside me instead. I muttered out loud, "If she wants to act like a boy, why shouldn't she?"

A shout from the bank echoed among the children, who squirmed closer to the opening of the trusses again, waving and pointing. "They're coming! I can see the logs!"

Tugging at muddy booted feet, Marion and I pulled them back to safer positions. As I tugged, I stared over the children and saw the heaving, racing logs, too. The spring logs were coming down Fifteen Mile Falls. I crouched low next to the children to see better, my hands on the collars of two wriggling little ones.

"My papa rides them!" proclaimed one child, a Hoyt by his shock of dark red hair. Bobby, I thought. The other children's voices, talking about their fathers too, rose to be heard over the roar of the river.

Where was Papa? I strained to distinguish logs from water. No man could ride the logs through the

Fifteen Mile Falls. Not anymore, not with the "short" pulp logs. Long logs, the ones from before I was even born, those were the ones the loggers rode. But even then, according to Papa, the loggers wouldn't ride them through the rough, rocky waters cascading southwest in the Falls. Well, some fools tried, most often drunk, and people talked about one of George Van Dyke's loggers who did it, way back, and landed in the river and hung onto a boulder until the other men rescued him, riding in a crude logger's pirogue, a narrow craft that only a real riverman could keep from spinning in the rapids. Still, that was in the old days, at least twenty years ago. Papa never rode logs in the Falls even then. He wouldn't even ride through the Falls on the wanagan, the raft with the cook shack at the end of the log run — the big workhorses would walk along the riverbank and ease the raft downriver, straining against the ropes and chains that reached out into the water. Papa would work the horses for this run, I guessed. So I peered to the side of the water, squinting into the rain, looking for men and horses on the riverbank.

Not yet.

The shouts of the children were louder than the crowd on the bank. Or at least closer, so I could hear them over the crashing water. Now the logs came in dozens, in hundreds, short and wild and dangerous, swinging and charging through the narrower, deeper section of water that swept toward the bridge. Some hit the banks under the bridge, making the wooden floor thump and quiver in response. They bounced, four to six feet long, ice on some of their edges, wet and slick, for they had been "peeled" upriver, and darkened on the grooved cut faces of their ends. They plunged under us in the dark water.

On the bank, two men held a rope that they'd fastened around Jimmy's waist as he leaned into the current and poked at logs that threatened to stick along the muddy, stony edge. I spotted Katy out of the store at last, hesitating by the group of adults, now some fifty or more. She seemed to realize she'd see Jimmy better from the bridge and hurried up to stand next to where I crouched with the children. We didn't speak; there was no point trying, over all the noise.

Now the real bulk of logs came heaving over the rocks on the thrust of water. In a moment, the river surface changed to logs, logs, logs, from one side to the other. Opposite Jimmy, two more men with peaveys on the other bank prodded and shoved.

The scent of wood, of cut pine and fir, wove into the thick face full of river smell that soaked the air.

It smelled like Papa. I looked again up the riverbank but saw no horses yet, no men. Numb with sound and cold and the endless thuds of logs on rock, river, and banks, I waited. My hands on the children's jackets clenched tighter, my arms aching.

Katy leaned close so I could hear, and said, "The logs will take hours. Maybe days. You can't hold on to those boys the whole time."

I stared at her. She was right, of course. But—but what if one of them fell in? Like Gratia. I started to answer, and she waved away the words. "I know," she said. "You're worried. I'm going to go get Mr. Simpson. Maybe he can close up the gap some."

Mr. Simpson, Marion's father, also was father of two of the boys in the huddle on the bridge. And he was a carpenter. I nodded to Katy, and she hurried off toward the crowd while I opened each of my hands, one at a time, to get the blood running in them again, quickly refastening on the children's jackets.

A long ten minutes later, Katy helped pull the children away from the edge while Mr. Simpson nudged a board into place across the gap. Nails from his pockets and quick strikes of a large hammer secured the board. Now a gap at the top and another at the bottom could still provide a view, but no children would fall.

Arms linked, Katy and I moved away from the shouting boys and stood near the end of the bridge, still a bit sheltered from the rain, watching Jimmy and the others urge the pulp logs back toward center river. A handful of log drivers, river men, wandered along the banks, too, peaveys in hand, shouting and grunting. Papa wasn't among them.

The wanagan, the raft with the blacksmith's gear and cook shack, might not even reach Waterford until the next day, or even a day later. And Papa could be even behind that, nursing the horses along the river edge, using their power to force stuck logs back into the rushing water. So when Katy said, "Let's go help my mother," I left the river with her. Maybe if the mass of logs moved fast enough, Papa might slip home for the night. I'd have to wait and see.

As we walked away from the river and the wet, talkative crowd pointing and waving, I saw two people that I hadn't seen before.

One was Henry Laporte, walking along the hill track above the village, barely visible but unmistakable, baskets humped against his shoulders, face toward the river. I doubted that he could see me from that distance, but it made me feel funny in my chest, knowing I could see him there.

The other was a man with a truck that had pulled

up on the road between the store and the river. The man, a black hat with wide brim shielding his face, stood on the running board of the truck, scanning the crowd.

Katy nudged me and said quietly, "It's the boss from the dam." The power company dam being built above the town, the dam that would close this part of the river so the logs wouldn't come through next spring.

What was he looking for? Or who? I shivered, and hurried with Katy up toward the store steps. That man carried a threat that I didn't understand, and didn't want to.

·✦·

Inside the store, I saw Mrs. O'Connor and her husband waiting on customers, dishing up noon meals:
baked beans with ham, big floured biscuits, slabs of
gingerbread. Katy and I wriggled back into aprons,
tying each other's sashes. We moved smoothly into
place next to Katy's mother, cutting, dipping, serving,
while her father took over the cash register.

In front of us the door flew open, hurled by a
gust of wind and rain. Dripping and coughing into
one hand, one of the men I didn't know stamped his
feet at the doorway, then pushed into the store, leaning against the door to shut it. He carried a sack of
mail and parcels, and a string-wrapped bundle of
newspapers. Mr. O'Connor made room by the cash

register for all of it, swept the envelopes aside into a bin, and put the packages on the wooden shelf that ran the length of the shop. With the packages he set aside the "reserved" papers. The rest became part of the display beside him. He never stopped ringing up purchases the whole time, and talked endlessly.

"And that's four gingerbread and a quart of beans," he rattled off, punching the round golden keys on the cash register. "Just bring back the plates when you've finished, please, Mrs. Willson. And would you like your newspaper now or later?"

"Later, please," Mrs. Willson decided, balancing an armful of plates and passing them along to a woman behind her that I didn't recognize.

"Yes, indeed," Mr. O'Connor chattered, "and what can I do for you, Hal Palmer?" He pushed a paper forward and Mr. Palmer took it. I ducked my head back to the gingerbread, slicing another careful row.

Mr. Palmer, who was a deacon at the church and also sexton for the cemetery, had thick white hair that curled around the edges of his cap. I listened to him with half my thoughts, the others resting on the man who was the dam boss, from the power company. Why was he looking at the people instead of the river? For that matter, why wasn't he at the dam site?

Mr. Palmer read aloud from the afternoon papers:

"Vermont for Real Yankees, that's the same as this morning's paper. A strike at the mill in Bellows Falls, just the time they'd do it with the wood coming downriver. Oh, a fire at the cobbler shop in Barnet. Can't do much damage with rain like this, can it? Still, you never know."

I moved closer to Katy for a moment and asked her quietly, "Why do you think the dam boss was at the river?"

She shrugged. Despite being an old man, at least as old as my grandmother, Mr. Palmer heard my question. "Eh? The dam boss? Looking for his men, most likely. Fire them if he sees them off the job in the middle of the day, you know. Right thing to do. If people won't work, why should they get paid?" He turned toward Mr. O'Connor. "Strikes, now, that's something I never had patience for. Take a man's money for work, and then when he needs you most, pull back and say you won't work more unless you get more money. Shame on them. They don't know what a good Yankee job is worth."

Oh. I thought about the people I'd seen at the river. I couldn't think of anyone that belonged at the dam instead; mostly it was schoolchildren, some parents and grandparents, people from the village watching the logs arrive and fill the river. Who would risk their job just to see? Being fired would be awful. My father would never let that happen to him, I knew. Now a worse idea hit me: Could someone fire him for being Indian or "French," even though he worked so hard?

Katy distracted me by asking her mother, "Do you want us to go up to the Bradley farm and get the eggs?"

So much happened in each day of the store, and it seemed the daily egg delivery hadn't come. Moments later, we were out of our aprons, out the door, and in the rain again, carrying a wooden crate, one handle each, headed out the river road to the Bradley place at the edge of the village.

Looking toward my own house, I felt guilty: Mama was doing wash of course, and I wasn't there to help. I was helping Katy's mother instead.

But Me-Mere could help Mama. And Mama said I could be at the river. What did it matter that I was at the store instead—or in fact, at the moment, out of the store and walking with Katy?

I looked up at the bit of the hill road I could see, but Henry Laporte was gone, of course. Before Saturday, I'd have to find him and tell him that I couldn't go up on the mountain this weekend after all. Probably he wouldn't mind. And maybe I'd go some other day, with Katy, too, if we felt like it.

All this flew through my thoughts in a short moment, and then I pushed it aside. I needed to tell Katy about Papa's visit, and Mama's condition. And I wanted to hear more about how Jimmy had told her he'd take her to the movie theater. Take us, that is. What movie would it be? How much would it cost?

For a rainy day, it surely was a busy one.

·✦·

Papa didn't come home that evening. Mama said it could be a week or more until we'd see him again — and even then, most likely just for a night. The log run, she said, was only going as far as McIndoe Falls this year, where the Connecticut Valley Lumber Mill stood, but to keep the logs controlled and clean up the ones that dodged ashore over those ten miles would still take time. And the weather had to hold calm enough, too. I tried to hide my disappointment. I was tired of a house of women.

Now that I knew Mama was expecting, I told myself to overlook her crabbiness. I saw my grandmother checking the pan in the oven, and after I set the table, I sliced some bread and offered to open a jar of applesauce. Mama said not to bother—with Papa not here, we could keep our supper simple. There would be less to wash up that way, too. So we each used a single bowl for our scalloped potatoes and mopped our dishes clean with our bread, and while Me-Mere filled the dishpan with hot water from the stove, I brought more wood from the shed, for the morning's tubs of washing.

After working with Katy all afternoon, I felt tired as a farm girl. Mama looked even more tired, though. She sat in the rocker, watching my grandmother and me, sipping from a mug of hot tea.

I dropped a last armful of kindling into the wood box and walked over to my mother. Awkwardly, I bent to kiss her cheek, catching the scent of her hair and a whiff of onions from her hands—but she lifted an arm to stop me.

"It's too hot in here," she said, "and you don't need to make a fuss. You're a good girl, Molly. I'm going to bed; you should too." She pressed the empty mug into my hand and, with a little push against my shoulder, cleared room to rise. I pulled back, hurt in spite of my effort to understand. She didn't look into my face, just walked out of the kitchen and up the stairs toward her bedroom.

Me-Mere took the cup from me, swished it in the

dishpan, and handed me the pan of water to empty outside. Out through the porch I went, one more time, and hurled the dishwater toward the vegetable patch. Under the rain clouds, the last of the daylight had failed, with fog swirling darkly, and a chill shook me. I hurried back into the house.

Me-Mere gripped my arm, holding me in place by the wide table a moment. "Let her be, Molly," she insisted. "She loves you. You know that." She squeezed harder on my arm, but I bit my lip and didn't answer. "Molly, listen to me. It's the little one's death, especially now that there's another baby coming. And each time she kisses you, she's"—Me-Mere paused, then finished as though she'd decided I was old enough to hear something important—"she's kissing Gratia, too."

I shivered. I couldn't help it. Mama kissing my cold, drowned sister, the one who haunted my bedroom? But in spite of myself, I heard truth in what Me-Mere was saying. Maybe when the new baby came, Mama could forget Gratia a little and love me a little more.

"*Olegwasi,*" said my grandmother, letting go at last. "Good dreams."

"Sleep well," I answered, not repeating the

Abenaki phrase. Instead I forced myself to nod at her as I escaped the kitchen. Over my shoulder I added, "See you in the morning. Comb out your hair and look pretty."

She nodded back, and I climbed the rest of the stairs, pushed past my parents' silent bedroom, and went into my own, shutting the door as quietly as I could.

Careful to hang my clothes, and remembering to brush the hem of my mud-stained skirt, I followed a nightly ritual to avoid scoldings from either Mama or Me-Mere. It was warm in my room, almost hot, from the kitchen heat. I lit the little bedside lamp. Its soft light wasn't really enough to let me inspect my face in the narrow pier glass. I wished for a full mirror over the dresser. But only Mama and Papa had one in their bedroom.

Close to the pier glass, turning slowly to try to see more of myself, I regarded the fit of the bodice I'd worn under my shift. It would do for a little longer, I concluded, for the thick cloth served well to smooth the outlines of my growing breasts. They were tender, warning me that the monthly cycle would soon enter its bleeding time. I reached to untie the strings behind my back, and as the cloth released I saw lines in my skin where the edges of the bodice had pressed and dug. From the dresser drawer I took a small jar of rose-scented cream my grandmother had made for me and smoothed it into the lines. Roses and the warmth of my hand against my chest stirred something I didn't understand, a sort of tension that shot in threads along my face, chest, thighs. Tentatively, I rubbed a bit of the rose cream on the softest part of my belly, then massaged more into my hands, which were dry from washing the supper dishes. All the while, I watched the narrow slice of reflection in the pier glass as I moved. I took off my two hair ribbons and combed my hair long and straight, surprised at how many tangles it had acquired without the usual snug braids to hold it all day. Then I turned down the wick of the lamp and let the light vanish. Belatedly, I thought of trying to write about the long day in my diary, but even the thought of that much more effort seemed too hard. Life was happening too quickly to write it down.

In the dark, I pulled my nightdress over my head and climbed into bed, discovering that Me-Mere must have been there—the hot water bottle she left had taken the damp out of the sheets. But it was too warm for my feet on this night, and I drew the flannel-wrapped bottle out and set it on the floor. I moved my feet to find a cooler patch of the sheets, tucked an arm under the pillow, and without even a good-night prayer, fell deeply asleep.

Despite the distant roar of the river and a faint awareness of its load of logs, I dreamed no river dreams, no Gratia or Papa in my night's eye. Only a cool hand on my hot face, and cool fingers against mine. Only a wondering, without form.

·✦·

Tuesday morning, in spite of the continued flow of pulp logs down the Falls, Mama sent me to school. One day off to see the log run was enough, she said crisply, cutting off my protest. I knew there'd be more to watch by the river, and people from away would come to see. But it was the last week of school, after all.

I didn't expect anything to be much different, other than just another four days of school to finish. But three things were different that day.

The first came soon after the bell had settled the school, younger children in the classroom to the right of the entrance, older ones to the left, with Katy and me and two other girls off in the corner, working to finish the mathematics book by the end of the week. Miss Webster came over and sat at our table, unusual in itself. She asked Susannah and Rebecca to move to the front bench and listen to the fifth graders read aloud. Then, dropping her voice, she looked back and forth between Katy and me and said, "Girls, I need to know your plans for next year."

We looked at each other, startled, and Katy spoke first. "We still have another year to graduation, Miss Webster."

The teacher, long face creased with concern, explained: "The two of you would be the only students for next year's grade twelve. But if you plan to teach, you see, you really should apply to the teachers' college in Montpelier this spring, so that in September you can begin your training there. I think, Kathleen, that you did say you wanted to teach?"

Half question, half instruction. Katy nodded, then protested. "But Miss Webster, couldn't I earn a teacher's certificate here instead?"

"I don't think that would be a good idea," came the firm reply. "You young ladies need a wider sense of where you belong in the world. I would like you to discuss this with your parents this week, and I will speak with you about it again on Friday. And"—she twisted sharply toward me—"Margaret, you have a gift in mathematics and perhaps in the study of natural history. You also have promise as a teacher."

"But I don't want to teach, Miss Webster," I protested.

"Yes? I am listening, Margaret. What is it that you prefer to pursue?"

A flash of warning from Miss Webster's eyes told me I had better not say the truth: that I would do anything to avoid becoming a teacher, being trapped in the role she filled. I would walk to Canada, or learn to sew straight seams, or even do the washing—no, not that. The idea of doing what my mother did daily shocked me. I stammered, "Would a gift in mathematics let me become, er, a doctor, Miss Webster?"

"No," she said immediately. "It would not. It would certainly be helpful, but I will not hide from you, Margaret, that the training in medicine is both difficult and costly, and I suspect your family would not support eight years of costly schooling for you. Am I correct?" She pressed on. "Medicine is also, I must add, a field in which women do not yet have a secure place, unless they enter through nurses' training. Would your inclination support your becoming a nurse, Margaret?"

"No!" I was sure, but hurried to repair my abrupt reply. "No, thank you, Miss Webster. I don't believe that nursing is my calling, ma'am."

The sharp brown eyes under the flying eyebrows inspected my mind as readily as my mathematics papers. "Well then," Miss Webster concluded, "if Kathleen applies to the college in Montpelier, I cannot imagine you would enjoy studying alone for the next year as the single advanced student here, Margaret. Think on this, please, and we will talk about it again on Friday. Thank you, girls, you may continue your work."

With a brisk nod, she stood and moved to the front of the classroom, shooing Susannah and Rebecca toward our table again. Under her gaze, we didn't dare whisper to the others what Miss Webster had talked about, but hissed, "At recess!" to them, and all picked up pencils to do our long division sums.

The second unusual thing happened at recess, while Katy and Rebecca and Susannah and I talked under the maple tree, sitting on the bench. Rebecca's little brother Joel ran past us and sang out, "Becky's gonna get cooties, sitting with a dirty Frenchy!"

Red-faced and clearly horrified, Rebecca leapt up and chased her brat of a brother, declaring, "I'll tell Mama on you, and she'll wash your mouth out with soap!"

Katy and Susannah told me not to worry about that stupid boy, and Susannah broke her last cookie in half and gave me a piece, the larger half, with raisins in it. But the school yard affection didn't take away the sting of the taunt. In fact, I felt like a liar: what would my friends and their brothers say if they knew I wasn't just a French Canadian, but Indian? For so many of them, Indians were just part of Western movies, where cowboys shot them. And Indians were savages, weren't they? I struggled to place such certain knowledge against the other kind of certainty, that my parents were the best parents in the world, that my family was different in a good way, Abenaki and "first in America" before even the Pilgrims came.

The sun in my eyes, weak though April made it, suddenly seemed too hot and bright, and a headache blossomed behind my forehead.

"I think I'll go inside," I said to the others. "I don't feel very well."

Walking away from their visible concern, I left them to sit under the tree and talk about me if they wanted to. I slipped back into the schoolhouse, pulled a chair out from the back table, and laid my head on my arms, nurturing the very real ache and a stomach that surged and clenched with uncertainty.

Things come in threes, they say.

That afternoon, while Miss Webster read aloud to us all from *The Peterkin Papers,* a knock at the door frame interrupted her. In the open doorway, through which a damp spring breeze had circulated since noon, two women stood in white uniforms, the neat striped caps of nurses on their heads. One, the older one, spoke as Miss Webster lifted a questioning eyebrow.

"Good afternoon, Miss, er, Miss Webster," the first stranger said quietly, consulting a slip of paper in her hand. "This is Nurse Williams"—a gesture to the woman beside her—"and I am Nurse Carpenter, from the district health office for the State of Vermont. I believe you have your report forms prepared for us?"

Miss Webster nodded as she stood. "Yes, of course, the students' heights and weights for your records. One moment, please."

Behind the wide, paper-stacked surface of her

desk, she drew open a drawer and extracted a small clipped bundle of forms. I could see the emblem of the state at the corner of the one on top, and Miss Webster's large, graceful signature.

She handed the papers to the first of the nurses, who thanked her and, with a practiced sweep of gaze around the classroom, continued, "Of course, we would like to conduct some further interviews with some of the more unusual students."

I met her frowning look at me and defensively crossed my arms over my chest. Katy slid her chair closer to mine with a low scrape on the floor. Miss Webster ignored the sound and said firmly to the nurse who'd spoken, "I'm afraid I don't permit interviews with my students individually. But you are welcome to return here at three, and I will meet with you and provide routine information if there is not enough in the records."

A long silent moment held a tense question: Who would determine the rules here, Miss Webster or this nurse?

Not surprisingly, Miss Webster took the round, at least for the moment. The nurse nodded, and her companion slipped backward into the hallway.

"We'll be here again at three, then," said Nurse Carpenter. "Thank you."

I was sure she shot one more look at me, and another at Katy, before she turned and left the building. The sound of the two sets of city-shoed feet on the porch steps echoed in the quiet classroom.

Miss Webster calmly reopened *The Peterkin Papers*. "And we continue with Elizabeth Eliza's story," she announced, and resumed reading aloud.

Very carefully, I tore a scrap of paper and marked on it a message to Katy: "Vermont for Real Yankees?" I passed it discreetly into her palm. She read the words, following my thought exactly, gave a tiny nod and wrote on the back of the paper, "My house after school."

I didn't dare pass a second note; Miss Webster was sure to notice. Instead, I gave an equally tiny nod and faced forward, paying as much attention as I could to the unreal adventures of the Lady from Philadelphia in the unfolding tale.

What if the cousins and uncles and aunts had not come to dinner on Easter and talked about the governor's plan? I might not have recognized the reason those nurses looked so closely at me and at red-haired, freckled Katy. As it came clear to me, even with the nurses gone from the schoolroom, the awareness of danger put a coppery scent into my nostrils, and the hair on the back of my neck rose.

Another hour and thirty-five minutes of school. And another three days of school beyond that. I wished it were longer, after all.

And the day after tomorrow, Thursday, would be my sixteenth birthday.

· ✦ ·

At first I couldn't sleep. So much was happening: the end of my father's winter in the woods, my mother expecting a baby, Miss Webster talking about school in Montpelier. Turning sixteen suddenly felt too soon.

And Gratia: the older I became, the further behind she was for me. *You can't be sixteen and believe in the ghost of a five-year-old sister,* I told myself as I pulled up the covers. I prayed, "God bless Mama and Papa and Me-Mere." Then I added a new part to my good-night prayer: "God rest Gratia, please. And God bless the baby."

There.

God, the God of the village and the church, loved little children. Everyone knew that. So God would watch over the baby, and if Gratia was an angel, she was with God.

Eyes closed, almost asleep, I felt a cold breeze suddenly across my pillow. *Not Gratia,* I insisted to myself. *Gratia's in heaven. Gratia's with God. Gratia is Some Place Else.*

I peeked from one eye. No glowing form in the corner, and no mysterious river scent either. The rising moon outside the window hung large in a pool of sky mist. The window—it was open a bit. That explained the cold air. Reluctantly, I left the warm bed to press the window down to the sill. I could see the shapes of dark hills beyond the village. Back in bed again, I thought about the hills, and Henry Laporte, and how I would tell him that I couldn't walk in his woods this weekend.

I glided from thinking in the darkness to a drift of dreams. Not Gratia this time, but the woods: I walked in the woods with Henry, as if it were Saturday after all.

"A basket begins with need, with hunger," he told *me as we walked up a steep bare hillside, cold and wet and slick underfoot. Gritty mounds of old snow huddled in hollows. My feet ached with cold.*

Henry went on, "Brother Beaver doesn't need a basket. He pulls his willow shoots down into his lodge for winter and weaves them there, to nibble when he needs them. Brother Fox is too quick for a basket. And he doesn't need to carry more than a mouthful." The basket boy in my dream stood facing me and tapped my chest. "Need is what the People have. Need is from the heart. I can teach you how to make a basket for whatever you desire."

In my dream I told him, "I don't know what I need. I don't know what I desire. So how can I make a basket?"

My hands in the dream waved in front of me, making a space between Henry and me. "We're different," my hands said, pointing back and forth between Henry's darker skin and muscle-roped wrists and my own indoor paleness. My hands said, "You're part of the real People, the real Abenaki. I'm not."

A fox ran past me, and a beaver crouched next to a tree, looking at me. In the dream, Henry said, "They know you, Molly. Brother Fox, Brother Beaver. Sister Hawk too. Look!"

And a powerful bird in speckled feathers swept down from the wet sky, knifing in flight over my head. A single feather spun in the air and settled on my palm. I held it out toward Henry.

He shook his head. "It's yours," he whispered. "She wants you to fly."

Holding the feather by the shaft, I watched the bird soar again, then reach the path of the frothing, tumbling river. Up rose the bird, circling over the water. It began to call out from the sky, and something in the water answered.

"The River." I touched one of Henry's hands, cool and smooth even in the dream. "Brother River? Or Uncle?" I struggled for the right words. Abenaki words.

"Not a person," Henry said. "A river is a place for fish, for animals, for people. This is Kwinitegok, Long River, Connecticut River. Listen to the river. You belong here too." Kwinitegok, a name that my grandmother used. And now Henry, in my dream. I strained to hear more.

But I could only hear the hawk, its thin high cry, as thin and strong as a baby's in the night.

And though I know there were more dreams that followed, the rest of them ran chill and hidden, until at last I surrendered to the darkness of the aging April night.

March comes in like a lion and goes out like a lamb. That's the saying, but for Vermont it should have said April.

Overnight, the weather changed. Wednesday morning opened with thick fog over the river and filling the village, the kind of fog that hides a bright sun in spite of the heat of it. An eerie brightness whitened the air. Mama and Me-Mere shooed me out the door — they were bustling into spring cleaning now that Papa would be home for good any day. So I didn't tell them about the boss from the dam or about the visiting nurses. Not about Miss Webster's questions either. Or the plan to go to the movies on Saturday with Katy and Jimmy. There was plenty of time ahead for that, at least. Asking too soon would just give them more time to think of reasons why I should be helping at home!

Morning dragged at school that day: an essay to write, and the last pages of the mathematics book with its tedious exercises to finish. But recess finally arrived. Rebecca and Susannah sat with Katy and me, listening to us talk about the new choices.

"I didn't know we could change schools this year." Katy bounced with excitement. "But when I told my father what Miss Webster said, he said it sounded like a good idea. And my mother said she'd like to see us with a larger group of girls, in town. She said we need more friends our own age."

Susannah complained, "Becky and I are almost your age anyway." She tossed her head crossly.

"But," Katy said, "you're not old enough to decide about changing schools, are you?" Her green eyes sparkled with excitement. "Molly, we'll need to make new clothes for town. I have a pattern for a pleated skirt, and Mama has three new bolts of fabric already."

I shook my head. "I can't. I'm not leaving Waterford yet. I don't want to go to Montpelier, and I don't want to teach anyway."

I was a gray cloud over Katy's enthusiasm. A gray cloud she didn't want.

"We're always together," she argued. "You've got to come to Montpelier. You're too good to stay here in this dinky little school anyway, Molly, you know you are. And teaching gives a girl independence and a living of her own. You never know when you're going to get married, you might need to manage on your own for a year or more."

"Married!" My voice rose, exasperated. "It's not about getting married, and it's not about being too good for here. This is where I belong! And my mother's having a baby, she'll need me to stay here and help her."

Nobody could argue with that. Susannah and Rebecca made agreeing sounds, asking about when the baby would come. Katy, though, just stared at me with her face growing red, her freckles dark against her cheeks.

"I can't believe what you're saying," she exploded. "You really won't come with me? After being best friends for all these years? You're not my best friend after all!"

Irish temper. I groaned and tried to interrupt. No use, though—in a whirl of skirt and stamp of boots, Katy leapt from the bench under the maple tree and nearly ran back into the schoolhouse, the door slamming behind her.

What could I do? Nothing. I sat and looked at my hands. The other two girls, embarrassed, said, "She'll get over it, Molly, don't worry," and hurried to talk about the upcoming picnic for the last day of school. *Let them talk without me,* I thought. *Nobody wants to hear my side. Nobody understands, not even my best friend. Life doesn't have the same choices for everyone.*

A breath of a whisper at my left ear said, "You're alive. You have all the choices that I don't have. Why not?"

I jumped and spun around. Nobody there. Who spoke? Was it — could it be — Gratia after all? Suspicious and embarrassed, I wanted to shout: *Little sister, if it's you, leave me alone!*

Under the stares of the other two girls, I fumbled at my shoulder, brushed it, and said, "Something bit me, I think." Even as I made up the white lie, the scent of river water seemed to drift through the school yard. In the background, the way it had been for weeks now, the river was pounding and rumbling. Faintly, the shouts of the men by the bridge echoed to the school yard.

For the first time, I eyed the school-yard fence with a wish that I was beyond it, all grown, past classes and teachers and exercises and such.

Maybe I was, after all, too old for the school in Waterford. But what good would it do to think about anything else? I wasn't a storekeeper's daughter, was I? My mother took in washing; my father rode the river and helped with summer haying.

Bitter as day-old coffee, I simmered in frustration. Only the bell for the end of recess took me back to my seat inside. Katy had pulled her seat apart from mine and sat focused on a history book, ignoring the three of us as we settled back into our chairs.

Some friend, I complained silently to myself. *Nobody understands.*

A rolled-up scrap of paper struck my ankle with a snap and a bite. I bent to pick it up. Shielding it from anyone's view, I smoothed it on my desk and read: "Roses are red, violets are blue, skunk cabbage smells, and Frenchies do too."

A flood of bitter and sour and hot and awful rushed through me, and I swept the note onto the floor, seized my satchel of books, and despite the stares of the others in the room and Miss Webster's rapid approach, hand outstretched to seize the bit of paper, I just plain ran out the door and down the street—not toward home, but toward the road west out of town, the road above the river.

Though I knew the woods must have people and animals in them, rushing from the school yard to the forest that lay between the village and the dam meant escaping into silence for me. An occasional call of a passing crow and the background hiss of the river, muted by the bare trunks of trees, held no words. Nothing hurtful. And though there would soon be robins proclaiming their territory, chickadees bouncing around, and the peepfrogs chorusing from every damp hollow, today's sudden sunshine only spelled the start of those warmer days. Patches of dirty old snow hunched to one side of the woods road. Frozen clumps of horse manure made the road hard to walk on, with its deep ruts and stretches of mud.

I hung my satchel on a broken-off branch and walked on without it. What trouble was I in for running out of school this way? I didn't care. For years, maybe forever, stupid rhymes about being French, and stupid jokes, flew around school. Always. And Mama and Papa taught me to ignore them quietly, not to tease back or say anything, just know it takes a stupid person to say a stupid thing—and a smart one to ignore it.

Today, though, everything seemed worse. Choices I hadn't expected. Katy expecting me to do things I couldn't possibly do. And the cold twist of April that made it all worse, with Gratia somehow talking to me in the daytime as well as at night.

Maybe I was crazy.

My dream from the night before, of walking in the woods with Henry, came back to me. Cautiously, I looked around: a fox? a beaver? No, I saw only the ratty end of winter. Not even a person to talk with.

After balancing on a slippery log at the side of the woods road and working my way past a long stretch of mud and manure, I stopped and sniffed. River smells, river sounds. Well, they were real this time. And Papa really had come out of the woods, even if he couldn't stay with us yet. And the powerful spring waters kept racing—the more I walked this woods road toward the dam, the closer the waters were. But Gratia's voice gave me doubts about spring, about water, about myself. Did Gratia hate me for being the sister still alive? Was Gratia's voice real?

Starting to walk again, edging carefully along in wet brown leaves that slimed the ground, I considered. Were there any other reasons to think I might be crazy? Voices, dreams, hauntings. Darkness underneath things.

Abruptly, I shrugged. Everyone has dreams. Even bad ones. Anger replaced worry: my life, my life today, was definitely unfair. I kicked at the leaves and stomped on a branch, hard enough to break it and spatter my skirt with mud.

The realization that I needed to return to school, apologize to Miss Webster, and get back to finishing the math book for the year eventually stopped me. In the distance an occasional bang of metal or wood and rumble of machinery told me I'd come more than halfway toward the dam site. For a moment I hesitated, thinking I might keep walking to go see it.

Then I turned and, with the soft spring sun on the back of my neck, headed back toward the village. I picked my satchel up as I went, and on the village road I scraped my shoes as clean as I could. Quietly, I walked back to school.

Just as I stepped through the school yard gate, a flash of white down the river road caught my eye and I paused, straining against the distance to see what was happening. Two women in white walked along the roadway. The state nurses from the day before. As I watched, they knocked at the almost never used front door of my own house.

I ducked quickly toward the school building, noting down the road the small shift of light that indicated the house door being opened. From that distance, I didn't think they could see the school yard, but if Mama or Me-Mere saw me outside school when I shouldn't be, there'd be terrible consequences! So in spite of being very curious, and worried all over again, I eased the schoolhouse door open, wiped my shoes once more on the mat, and tiptoed, head down, to set my satchel by my chair before walking unhappily up to the front of the room.

Miss Webster didn't rise from the seat behind her desk, though she paused in marking the stack of papers in front of her. "Mar-ga-ret," she said slowly, one syllable at a time. "Take your seat, please."

"I'm sorry, Miss Webster," I began.

"Take your seat," she repeated without looking up. "When you and Kathleen have completed your mathematics exercises, you may both bring them forward. Thank you."

Nobody in the classroom looked up; thirty faces stayed in position, showing they were working.

But as I slipped at last into my own seat, I noticed that Katy had moved her chair back into position next to mine. She pushed the mathematics book toward me, pointing at the next section of problems, and without looking up, brushed one hand against mine before we both took our pencils and resumed the figures.

The nasty scrap of paper was gone from the floor.

·✦·

Katy and I walked home from school together. Our satchels were light, with mathematics and history textbooks no longer in them, only our essays to complete for the last day of school—which would also be my sixteenth birthday. Without talking about the earlier parts of the day, we linked arms and quietly, slowly strolled in the sunshine. A chill wind rolled down from the hills, but it still seemed like spring.

"What are you bringing Miss Webster on the last day?" I asked Katy.

She shrugged. "Probably my mother will give her maple syrup again. She liked it last year. What about your mother?"

"Apple jelly, I think. That's what we mostly have in the cupboard." I paused, then said, "You could come for supper tomorrow night. It won't be fancy or anything, but Mama is good with baking, and I think she'll make a pound cake."

Smiling faintly, Katy agreed. "And I'll bring your birthday gift. I don't want to bring it to school with me — you'll see why." She winked, the "Irish" coming back into her. "Sweet sixteen and never been kissed," she teased.

"Well?" I demanded. "You haven't been kissed either! Or" — I could be a little "Irish" too — "has Jimmy already kissed you?"

"No!" she squealed, dropping my arm and giving me a quick pinch on the back of my hand. "I haven't even gone out with him yet! And you're coming too on Saturday, aren't you? So everything will be good."

I agreed. "I have a quarter ready. What are you going to wear?"

We had just agreed to both wear our blue sweaters when we reached the road down to the river. "See you later," we told each other. And a few minutes later, ducking under a budding, too-long branch of apple tree by the door, I stepped into our kitchen.

My mother, looking hot and tired and cross, stood by the stove stirring the copper wash boiler. The thud of a closing door suggested my grandmother had just retreated. The floor gleamed wet and clean, and before I even had time to set down my satchel, Mama called out, "Thank goodness you're here! Take your shoes off before you come in! No, wait, don't come in yet, there's a basket of wet sheets on the porch; hang them on the line. Be careful!" Then, with a quick glance toward the stairs, "Hurry, Molly! I need you to peel potatoes. Your father may be home for supper."

I ducked away from her whirlwind of instructions, seized the heavy basket of wet sheets, and headed for the clothesline in the backyard. One moment I was a whole person, planning an afternoon with my friends. And the next moment, I was Mama's assistant, feeling like a ten-year-old who wants to say, "I won't!"

Life was not just unfair, I decided. It was also confusing.

We waited that night for Papa, but he didn't come, one more unfair part of my day. I wished I dared to stomp on the floor or at least complain. Mama's tight, short words and Me-Mere's warning glare fenced me in with my own frustration. We finally ate a late supper, just the three of us. Me-Mere and I ate in a conspiring silence, not wanting to start Mama into either instructions or tears. Knowing about her condition kept us gentle, but still, I wished my mother could be more like she used to be, at least be more like a friend if she couldn't act like a mother. Finally, with slices of apple pie in front of us and hot tea, Mama seemed to come back to herself for a moment and asked me, "How was school?"

"Good." It was a lie, but how could I admit I'd run out of the classroom? For protection, I added, "We finished all our books, and I need to finish writing something tonight. Just one more day and then the picnic, remember?"

She pushed back some long dark hair that had come loose from her braids, coiled atop her head. "I remember. And your birthday tomorrow. I remember that too. I'm only expecting," her voice rose, "not feeble-minded!" Me-Mere and I froze, but it was a short moment of heat, and Mama calmed and continued, "Perhaps your father is coming tomorrow for your birthday supper, so clean your room this evening please, young lady."

"I will," I promised. Cautiously I asked, "And who came to call today, Mama?"

She and Me-Mere grimaced at once. "Mrs. Beck

with two weeks of wash. Oh, and two nurses from Montpelier, with a hundred nosy questions."

"About me?"

Mama looked startled. "No, not about you, Molly." Her hand dropped protectively to her belly. "About the baby. When it's due, and everyone's health." She eyed my grandmother with irritation. "If certain people took better care of themselves, they wouldn't cough in front of company."

On cue, my grandmother cleared her throat and gave two short, barking coughs that rattled into a spasm. "It's just the change in weather," Me-Mere said when she'd caught her breath.

"Well, you made the nurses worried," Mama retorted. "They even wanted to measure around me, to see how the baby is growing."

"And you let them, didn't you?" Me-Mere snapped back. So that was the extra tension in the room: the two of them disagreed on how to handle these strangers, and the heat of the day's washing on top of the heat of the disagreement fed the irritation in the room.

Clearing my place quickly, I excused myself to go upstairs. Maybe if I just kept quiet, they'd leave me out of their argument. Those state nurses asking questions in my own home scared me, though. They worked for the governor, didn't they? Vermont for real Vermonters . . . could they send our family back to Canada or something?

Oh, Papa, come home soon again, I wished fervently. As I hurried toward the stairs, I saw the emptiness of the hallway: no sage; no baskets on the shelves; and the big, dark family photo was gone, too. A faint scent of beeswax made me notice the waxed floor and steps, in time to slow down and not slip. A plain blue vase stood on the small table by the front door, neatly centered on a lace mat.

It looked like anyone else's front hall now. Did it look that way to the nurses? Or had they known anyway, from my mother's small dark face, that we were not the "Vermonters" that the governor wanted in his state?

The twenty-fourth of April, a windy, raw day, was my sixteenth birthday. I woke with the hope that my father would be home, knew right away from the sounds of the house that he wasn't here, and scrunched my eyes shut again for a moment, to wish really hard that he would somehow slip away from the river for my birthday supper.

After that moment, the day belonged to "last day of school and hurry up!" Breakfast was bread and jam and coffee, standing up, so as not to make a mess. At school there were books to sign back onto the school list, school library books to sort for Miss Webster, chalkboards to be washed, and everything in the classroom needed a final cleaning. The oldest boys washed the floor; each of us students cleaned our desk and chair; Miss Webster barely even gave us recess.

In the short break outdoors, Katy and Susannah and Becky and I huddled near the building to escape the sharp wind. Katy's cheeks and nose turned bright red with the cold, and I kept my hands tucked under my arms for warmth.

Susannah, irrepressible and bubbling, told us her family would take the train to Boston next week to visit relatives and buy leather. Her father was a cobbler, and though cash stayed short in the village, trade always sustained her family. I wondered how he could buy leather, though, with so few people actually paying. Mama hardly ever received her two dollars for wash lately.

Still, it didn't seem polite to ask, so I mostly just listened. Then Becky asked Katy and me, "So will you do what Miss Webster said? Are you going to school in Montpelier next year?"

Katy nodded, excited. "I talked with my parents and they said Miss Webster is right, a teaching certificate from Montpelier will be much better than just graduating from Waterford. I'm picking berries all summer and I'll put the money aside, and my father can help." She turned to me and asked, "Molly, what did your mother say? Did she say you can go?"

"I didn't ask her. My father's not home from the woods yet," I added quickly, as if that was the reason. The others all nodded. My throat felt thick, knowing I didn't want to leave Waterford anyway, didn't want to tell Mama what Miss Webster had said. Still, if I didn't, someone else might mention it to my mother. Miss Webster might do it herself. If I didn't tell Mama soon, it would seem like lying.

Right away, Becky asked about my birthday instead: "Are you having a party?"

"No." I waved a hand casually. "I'm too old for that, really. Just a family supper." And because Becky looked so disappointed, I added, "But Katy and I are going to the movies in St. Johnsbury on Saturday!"

When the others found out Jimmy Johnson had asked Katy, the teasing started. "Katy and Jimmy sittin' in a tree, K-I-S-S-I-N-gee!" Susannah sang in a whisper. She giggled. We all did, while Katy shook her head to say no, but laughing.

"And Molly, did I tell you," Katy injected, "Jimmy says Eddie Beck is coming too, so we'll be a full car."

"Eddie Beck? I haven't seen him in ages. Is he working on the farm?"

"No," she told me, "he's working at the new

dam. But Jimmy and Ed are still best friends, so he's coming along."

Becky asked if there was room in the car for one more — or for two, with a quick look at Susannah. Katy said she doubted it, but promised to ask anyway.

I spent the rest of the day worrying about one thing after another, so I hardly heard Miss Webster half the time. I worried about finding Henry Laporte to tell him that I couldn't go to the woods with him on Saturday. And I worried about whether Papa was safe on the river drive, and whether he'd be home for supper and cake. And I still hadn't told my parents what Miss Webster suggested, which somehow I had to tell them, even though I knew we couldn't afford for me to go away to school in Montpelier.

With so much to worry about, I decided that I needed to grow out of listening to Gratia. She was just a little girl when she died. She never had to worry like this.

Inside the school, pushing Gratia away was easy, because the sound of the river didn't come into the classroom. But when that school day ended, I stood outside alone in the damp April air. Gray clouds scudded overhead, and the scent of rain and mud and horse pressed against me. I was too different — me with my dead older-younger sister, French Canadian parents who were Abenaki too, and look at me, good in math of all things, not what girls should be like anyway.

I shivered. *Gratia, if you're my guardian angel, where are you now?*

And though Katy walked as far as my road with me, she needed to go to her own house before supper, and she promised to be back at six. I skidded down the muddy road, blocking out the roar of the river as best I could, and said hello to Mama at the kitchen door. Then I told her I would be back in an hour to help with supper, and with only a raised eyebrow, she let me go.

Where would Henry Laporte be on a cold, windy April afternoon? This was my moment to find him, to clear the way for my Saturday plans with Katy.

Buttoning my coat all the way, I walked slowly through the village, careful to stay on the walkways where I could. A glow from the library windows beckoned, but that would have to wait for some other day. I walked past O'Connor's Store and the post office. The sound of the river and the thud of logs against the stone bridge footings filled the air. A group of older boys and a man I didn't know stood below the bridge, pike poles in hand, poking occasionally at logs that bounced toward shore. I saw the ends of a few of them, bouncing above the water, which was high, covering the boulders in a brown froth. But the river itself wasn't covered with logs by any means. The main log run must still be upriver. I doubted that Papa was close enough to come for my birthday supper.

Gratia's voice teased me: "Pity party, pity party, who'll pour the punch?"

I swatted at my ear, as though the inner voice were a fly or hornet. Dark as the four o'clock clouds, I scowled at the water, climbed onto the bridge to watch for a moment, and scanned the hills. Fog hung across the hilltops and sent wisps across the stretch of leafless trees. Hard to believe they'd turn green, ever.

This time I had no sight of Henry Laporte up on the roadway, and I left the bridge, walking back through the village. The damp length of my skirt slapped against my legs, and the wind kept catching at it, so I slowed down and held it with one flattened hand. Tugging my coat down lower helped keep the skirt from flying. I walked past my own road and on westward, to where I'd seen Henry turn toward his house that hid beyond the fields.

Luck at last turned my way, for a scuff of boots made me turn and look down the west road again.

I saw him coming from the woods road that led to the dam.

This time he had no baskets, wore no pack, carried nothing that I could see. Hands in his pockets, he walked toward me, giving a short nod as I looked at him. When he came close, he quietly said, "Hi," then took a hand out of his pocket and held out to me a small leaf. I opened my hand and reached forward.

His hand was cool as it brushed my fingers, setting the leaf gently onto my palm. I squinted at it, uncertain.

"What is it?"

"Yarrow." He looked pleased.

"Is it for something?"

"Mmm." Tipping his head sideways, looking into my face a moment, then back down at the leaf, he said softly, "Tea. Sure. But mostly, today, just spring, you know? I mean, it's growing."

"Oh. Spring." I looked at the leaf longer, unsure whether to close my hand over it. I asked him, "Do you want it back?"

"You can keep it."

So I put it into my own pocket, carefully, gently, so he wouldn't feel like I was crushing it or anything. It was hard to say the next part, but I started: "About Saturday."

He stood very still, looking at me. I wished he'd say something else, but he just waited.

"I can't go this Saturday after all," I rushed to say. "And Sunday I'll have to help my mother." I felt so bad that I suddenly said something I hadn't planned: "Maybe Monday afternoon though. After the wash is done, about three o'clock."

For a moment longer, he stood still, then lifted his head a bit. In spite of being short for a boy, he was taller than I was, and he could look into my face without straightening up all the way. "All right," he said simply. "And your friend?"

"Maybe." I hadn't thought about that. I'd ask Katy later.

Henry nodded, putting his hand back into his pocket. "See you Monday afternoon, then. About three o'clock, here?"

"Good." The relief came out in my voice, and again he looked at me, this time a question, but I pushed past the moment and just said, "Good, see you then. Bye!"

"Bye."

Though I headed directly back toward the village and didn't turn around to look back at him, I had a feeling he watched me for a few minutes before going toward his own house. But he walked so quietly that

I couldn't be sure. And I didn't want to turn, afraid I'd feel so guilty about going to the movies Saturday that I'd start trying to explain to him. At the same time, the way he'd just said "all right" made everything easier. I almost wished I was walking in the woods with him sooner, for the niceness of it.

Anyway, it was done. One less thing to worry about.

The afternoon suddenly dimmed as the sun slipped behind the hill, and I realized my hour was more than used up. I quickened my steps, thinking again: *It's my sixteenth birthday. Will Papa come home?*

Just as I reached the house, I heard a call from down the road, and there was my father, swinging down from a truck, calling my name. At the same time, Katy appeared, walking from the store, a brown paper bag in her arms. And the kitchen door swung open, with my mother leaning out, the unmistakable aroma of chicken pie drifting toward me.

It was, after all, a joyous birthday supper.

· ✤ ·

Alone in my room after Katy had gone home and my parents and grandmother were asleep, or nearly, I spread out my birthday gifts on my bed.

Katy's gift to me was a store-bought stationery set: pink paper decorated with roses, matching envelopes, a ribbon tying them together, and all fitted neatly into a shining pink box. "Best friends send the best letters," her card said. I smoothed the silky cover of the box and imagined sending letters to Katy in Montpelier the next fall. My parents could never send me away to school, I was sure already. Why tell them Miss Webster's message? It would only make them sad. If I kept the message to myself, I would be the only one sad — when Katy left town and I stayed here. Would Montpelier really be a better place to study? So far away, and such a big town, a city really, the state capital. No, it was impossible. Katy must know, must understand by now, and that was why she gave me the letter paper.

From my mother and father came a silver locket, one I knew my mother treasured. It hung on a new chain, and inside were two tiny pictures: one of Mama as a young woman, dark hair loose and flowing, half a smile on her carefully closed lips, and one of Mama and Papa from when they married, Papa in a suit, with a surprising mustache. Even in the photograph his eyes sparkled with laughter. I held the locket open a moment, then carefully closed it and fastened the chain at my throat. In the narrow pier glass it shone, and I let my hair down, turning back and forth to try to see my entire face at once. Did I look like Mama at my age?

My grandmother's gift surprised me the most. I thought she'd give me a woven sweetgrass basket or some other Abenaki traditional present. So when I unfolded the tissue paper and found a delicate embroidered satin bag, an evening handbag in cream satin edged with dark brown cord, it was so lovely that I could hardly thank her! And inside was a neatly folded dollar bill.

"Someday you'll have many more," she teased. "If you don't spend them all!"

I unfolded the dollar bill and fingered it, wondering whether she was right. My aunts and uncles always seemed to have money, with their shining automobile and store-bought clothes. Our family wasn't that way, though. So wouldn't I be more like my own family when I grew up?

This struck me as too much fancy, even for day-dreaming, and I put my gifts aside and slipped into bed, where there was no hot water bottle, as the house still held the heat of the day's washing.

But I couldn't sleep. Friday's picnic, predictable and customary, didn't hover on my mind. But Saturday afternoon at the movies, with Katy and Jimmy and Ed Beck — that was something so new and amazing that I kept thinking about it. Other families went to the Palace Theatre, or the Star Theatre, from time to time, to see the new Mickey Mouse cartoon or a romantic movie with Greta Garbo or Douglas Fairbanks. But not our family!

Even more than wondering about the movie, I wondered about riding in a car with my friends.

Would Katy and I sit in the backseat together? If she sat in the front seat with Jimmy, I'd be sitting with Ed in the back! And what would he expect? But he hadn't invited me—Katy had. So that's not a double date or anything. Then again, what if he thought it was?

On the spot, I determined to wear long sleeves, a thick sweater, and my longest skirt. I certainly didn't want Eddie Beck trying to hold my hand!

I fell asleep in the middle of sorting this out, and dreamed of green leaves on the trees, of warmer days, of a cool set of fingers brushing across mine.

And woke to Mama's call of "Breakfast!" with the house so unexpectedly warm that I almost thought my dream was true, and looked to see if someone touched my hand. But it was only a dream. And not even a dream of Gratia this time.

"Molly!" came the call in two voices at once, Mama and Me-Mere, and I jumped from the covers, calling, "Coming!" The school picnic was today and—a quick glance out the window confirmed— sunshine and a clear sky meant we'd have it outdoors in the school yard, with a few final speeches, then a lunch, and at last the end of school for the spring. Glory! Spring and summer and all erupted in my chest, a May feeling instead of an April one, and I tugged on my clothes and nearly flew to the bustling kitchen.

"You're late," Mama said crisply as she set oatmeal and a mug of coffee in front of me. "Don't dawdle."

"Where's —"

"Back on the river hours ago," Me-Mere answered. "It might be weeks until he's back, after the logs are all out and stacked at the mill in McIndoes. Don't talk now, just eat."

On impulse, I asked, "Mama, can you come to the picnic?"

She brushed my invitation aside with an exasperated wave of both arms at once: "And who'd be taking in the washing, then? Your grandmother alone? Don't be asking foolish questions. Go, and"— for a moment she actually smiled at me —"go have a good time. Now hurry!"

I seized the lighter moment to finally ask: "Katy wants me to go with her to a movie Saturday afternoon, Mama — so she won't feel shy about going with the others. Jimmy Johnson can drive us. Mama, may I go? Please? I could help all morning with the wash!"

"Just to help Katy, is that why you want to go?" Mama teased, and I grinned to hear her saying something that wasn't crabby or cross. She pushed a wrapped plate of cookies for the picnic toward me and swept me out the door, laughing.

"Go! Go to school! And, yes, you can go see the movie!" As the door swung shut I heard her repeat to Me-Mere, with another laugh, "Just to help Katy O'Connor!"

·✦·

The last morning of the school year, complicated by
some parents and too many presentations, sped past.
At noon I sat outside with Katy, Susannah, Becky —
and Miss Webster and Mrs. Simpson, who had
brought the sandwiches for everyone. We watched
the younger children enjoy the games: hopscotch,
tag, blindman's bluff. With nobody actually graduating, morning speeches had been short and only a few
mothers attended, mostly leaving right after lunch.
It felt strange now to sit with the grown women,
talking.

Miss Webster asked, "What are the older boys
doing this spring? I haven't heard from Edward Beck;
is he working on the farm with his uncle?"

"No, ma'am," Katy filled in. "He's at the dam. So are the Willson twins." They were a year older.

"Ah, that's nice. It's good to have well-paid jobs here, isn't it, Mrs. Simpson?"

"For as long as they'll last," Marion's mother agreed. "Another year at the most, I believe. Maybe less."

"Oh, that long?" Miss Webster's pleasant face showed she was both surprised and interested. "I didn't realize it would take so much time to complete the dam. I thought it was more than halfway done."

"Oh, yes, it's nearly three-quarters, I would say," Mrs. Simpson agreed. "But the water won't rise up all at once, and there's still work moving houses and the cemetery, you know. What I understand is, we'll have our new lake complete by next spring. And even then, there's roadwork to be done, with the highway moved and all."

Katy inserted, "Jimmy Johnson's working at the dam too, Miss Webster. And Sarah Stewart is one of the secretaries at the power company office."

"My goodness! I'm glad to hear that," the teacher responded. A wail from one of the small children interrupted us, and Mrs. Simpson and Miss Webster walked over to see what had happened.

I took advantage of the moment to ask Katy,

"What time are we leaving tomorrow for the movie?"

"At one. Jimmy's working in the morning, then he'll pick up Eddie and then me, and then you. What are you wearing?"

We agreed to "almost match" with our blue sweaters over white blouses, checked skirts, and necklaces. I could wear the locket and chain from my birthday. Susannah and Becky looked envious. There wasn't room in the car for them, Katy said firmly. I said I was sure Mama's permission needed definite times.

"What time do you think we'll be back?"

Katy guessed, "Five, maybe. Or maybe five thirty. Better tell your mother six, just to be safe. It's a double feature, you know!"

Everyone in school talked about the movies, even if they didn't go. Saturday's matinée would be a Mickey Mouse cartoon and then a new movie, about the Great War: *All Quiet on the Western Front*.

"It won't have any of the big movie stars, will it?" I wondered.

"No, not even Mr. Fairbanks. But I think one of the actors is a little bit famous, Lew Ayres."

"Why are you going to a war movie?" Becky

asked. "Isn't there anything else you could see? Does the Palace Theatre have anything with movie stars?"

"Yes," Katy confirmed, then lowered her voice. "It's a Greta Garbo movie. But it's about, well, a lady of the evening — you know what I mean?"

I was shocked. A movie about a prostitute? "Here in Vermont? At the Palace?"

"I know." Katy winced. "That's why we're not going there. I don't even see how it could be a romance. Unless someone saves her and falls in love with her, maybe."

"Wow."

We reflected on the possibilities. Miss Webster came back to sit with us while Mrs. Simpson took the crying child inside to bandage his skinned knee.

"So, young ladies," my teacher said as she began the question I'd dreaded, "have you considered your future? Susannah, Rebecca, you may help with that jump-rope game over by the tree now." The two younger girls left slowly, and Katy and I waited until they were far enough away to not be listening in.

"I've talked with my parents," Katy said, "and they gave me permission to apply to the school in Montpelier. Do I write a letter?"

Miss Webster shook her head. "No, I have an

115

application form. You can take it home with you today. And what about you, Molly?"

I began to try to explain that I just couldn't go but was interrupted. It was the nurses again, the ones from Montpelier. They stepped into the school yard and began to talk with the smallest children, the ones playing hopscotch by the gate. I saw them look across at Katy and me, and I froze.

In a swirl of irritation, Miss Webster swept across the yard and in her clear, crisp voice said, "I beg your pardon. I believe I've explained that we don't permit interviews with the students. May I assist you?"

As before, it was the older nurse who answered. "I'm afraid we are required by the legislature to further document the backgrounds and families of the children attending school here, Miss — er, Miss Webster. It is our assignment from the governor himself."

"Then you may do so with me, inside," our teacher said firmly, and swept the nurses into the classroom with her. Over her shoulder she called, "Miss Ballou and Miss O'Connor, you will supervise the school yard until it is time to line up at two o'clock, when I will dismiss the school."

A quick glance up at the clock on the church tower told us that would be in about half an hour. Becky and Susannah came over right away to ask about the nurses, but Katy shrugged. "They were here before, remember? Probably they just need the class list or something." I kept my doubts to myself. Together, the four of us moved closer to the hopscotch game, then intervened to straighten out the rules in the boys' game of tag. Conversation was impossible; with Miss Webster not watching, everyone played harder and louder. Even when Mrs. Simpson came out with the little boy with the bandaged knee, the others didn't quiet down.

I saw the nurses through the window, and they were still inside the classroom when Miss Webster came out to dismiss school. What did it mean? Yet there wasn't time to think about it, as the rush of children swept out the gate. Katy and I moved to the back of the group, and I felt a hand on my shoulder.

"You'll stop by over the summer and let me know as your plans mature," my teacher said firmly.

"Yes, ma'am."

Her unexpected smile made me feel more guilty than ever: I would have to tell Mama what the teacher had said. Leaving town like that just couldn't happen for me, I was sure.

I hurried to catch up with Katy, and we sat on the steps to O'Connor's Store, sun on our hair, hands without books, the next day's trip to town to consider.

I grinned at the way Katy was saying "Jimmy says" and "Jimmy told me." For Katy, maybe tomorrow really was a date after all!

So the long vacation began, without a doubt the strangest spring and summer of my life. But I didn't know that then. All I knew was, when I saw two woven baskets for sale inside the store and realized Henry Laporte must have brought them, two feelings mixed in my chest all at once: guilt, of course, for going to the movies with Katy and the others on the day when Henry and I had planned to walk first, and an odd quiver of excitement. April was almost over. Good things might lie ahead.

·✦·

I left Katy at about four o'clock, knowing I should go home and offer to help with washing or supper. But I didn't want to yet. *Let me have just one more hour of feeling the freedom of the end of the school year,* I told myself. Besides, concern over the nurses visiting the school simmered in the back of my mind, and I decided to peek and see whether they were still with Miss Webster. So I walked past the turn to my house, to reach the school. From the road I could see the lights were out, the big doors shut. They must all be gone.

I decided to walk just a little farther in the warm sunshine. I wasn't exactly thinking about Henry, but

I walked as far as the place where the Laporte farm road turned off the main road, then stood a moment looking across the wet field. I could smell the heated soil, the beginnings of growth. It smelled good. Farther down the main road, where the road to the dam began, I spotted someone walking. *It must be Henry,* I thought.

Instantly I felt embarrassed. He would think I was looking for him again, after talking the day before. I didn't want him to think I was "after" him. I stepped off the road and ducked behind a cluster of cedars, then stepped a bit farther, beyond a pile of stones. There, nobody would see me now. I found a dry stump and sat quietly, listening. Even though I was a town girl, I could imagine what a "real" Indian would do at a moment like this. Quiet, barely breathing, I waited. I heard boots scuffing gently along the road. *There now,* I thought, *he's making the turn toward his own house.*

A clatter of an engine and the rattling of stones and sand from the road signaled a truck or automobile coming toward the corner, from the same direction that Henry—if it was in fact Henry—had walked. Brakes squealed, and the vehicle stopped somewhere near my hiding place. The rank smell of gasoline smoke reached me, and I covered my mouth and nose with a handkerchief pulled from my pocket.

"Young man! Come here, please," called a woman's voice over the rumble of the engine.

I couldn't hear footsteps, but I heard Henry's voice somewhere beyond the vehicle, quiet but clear. "Ma'am?" he said in a low voice.

"Young man, what is your name?"

I recognized the tone of command, the crispness of the out-of-town voice. It was one of the state nurses! I crept carefully around the stones to peek through the cluster of cedar, staying low to the ground. My skirt dragged, and I carefully drew it close to me. I could see the gleam of an automobile, and enough through the window to be sure both nurses were in it. I crouched lower, where I couldn't actually see the vehicle—and so I was sure that nobody could see me either.

Very slowly, much more slowly than his usual calm tone, I heard him respond: "My name is Henry, ma'am." He made himself sound slow-witted somehow.

"Henry what?"

There was a long pause. And I heard the older nurse snap at him, "It's not a difficult question. What is your family name, young man?"

"Laporte, ma'am."

"There you are, you see, you can answer me, can't you? Now, where do you live?"

The sharp edge to the woman's voice bit the air, and I wished I could see more. What was Henry doing? I could hear something else. The older nurse was talking now to the other one, so her voice, aimed in my direction, came clearly. "Write it down, Miss Williams. No, not *L-o*, write *L-a*, it's a French name. Laporte, with an *e* on the end. Good. Mark it as *farm*. Henry, what is your father's name?"

Ah, he was even slower now. I strained to hear him say softly, "Papa."

I wanted to giggle. What a way to resist the questions!

"No," sharply, "his real name." Now the voice was sugary and coaxing. "What do the other men call him?"

I heard Henry clear his throat and then say, "They called him Samuel, ma'am. But he's gone."

"Gone? What do you mean, gone? Speak up. Gone away, or gone dead?"

"Gone away, ma'am."

I could hear satisfaction in the nosey woman's voice as she ordered the other nurse, "Write that down, *his father ran off.* We'll come back to this one later. Young man, tell your mother the nurses will be coming to see her next week, do you understand?"

"Yes, ma'am," I heard.

As the car pulled away, I heard one more direction from the older one to the younger: "Mark it down, I said. *Slow-witted. French!*"

I smiled to myself. Henry's father was only "gone" like mine, gone to the winter woods, could even be home already if his part of the logging was done for the year. But the nurses wanted to hear something bad, so they twisted the words. I was learning a lot about what an outsider could assume.

I waited while the racket of the automobile faded. I should be able to hear Henry walking away, shouldn't I? Maybe he was already partway down his farm road. After another moment of hearing nothing, I stood cautiously and tiptoed to the edge of the dark clump of cedars.

And jerked to a stop, more embarrassed than ever. For Henry was standing at my side of the road, a basket in one hand, the other arm half extended to help me across the soiled strip of old snow between me and the roadway.

He smiled at my dismay and pointed down into the grainy snow. I saw my boot prints clearly there.

"But how did you know it was me?" I fumbled.

He smiled the rest of the way. "Not that many people come walking toward the woods, and you've been here before in the late afternoon. I guess I just thought maybe it was you."

Ignoring his hand, I stepped back across my own prints and stood on the road, shaking twigs and such from my skirt. Without looking up, I said, "I wasn't trying to eavesdrop."

"I know," he said calmly. "I saw you before the car came along. You were smart to get off the roadway."

Now I did look into his face. "They're state nurses," I warned him. "From the governor's office. I think they're looking for Abenakis, and French Canadians, and even Irish. I think they're dangerous!"

"I think you're right," he agreed. "So you should go home and tell your grandmother and your mother. Tell them not to talk to the nurses. I'm going home to tell mine."

Good. He wasn't going to ask me why I'd been near his farm road. "They already visited my house," I told him, more worried than ever. "I'd better get home right now."

He nodded, and moved out of my way.

"Wait," I said. "How do you know about my grandmother and my mother?"

He grinned. "Your grandmother walks in the woods all the time," he pointed out. "And she has the best garden in the village, no matter what you need it for. Matter of fact," he said, laughing, his eyes lit up with mischief, "I might have given her a few plants for it myself!"

I laughed, too. Of course!

He headed down the farm road, and I headed back into the village, hurrying; it was nearly suppertime, and also the air was suddenly cold, as the sun sank behind the hills. I needed to tell my mother and my grandmother that the governor's threat had taken shape, right here in Waterford.

What could the nurses do to us? I wasn't sure. But it felt good to know that other people besides my own family realized they brought some kind of risk and menace. I wished my father would come home again soon. He needed to know about all this, too.

In spite of the sense of danger, I felt lighter of heart as I half ran back into the village. An early-rising moon clung faint and thin in the eastern sky, a whisker of white arc there. Faint pink colors from the last of the sun beyond the hill reflected across the sky too. Spring hung in suspense, just beyond the evening's chill.

Papa did not come home that night, of course. It was too soon. Still, I told my mother and grandmother that the nurses were still in town, and we all worried together.

· ✦ ·

By noon on Saturday, after standing over the steaming washtubs with Mama and Me-Mere all morning, and hanging wash from the lines until I thought my arms would turn to rubber, "mud season" seemed to me the dirtiest, most hard-working part of Vermont spring. Now that Mama's condition could be talked about, she and Me-Mere kept asking me to do more things for the sake of sparing Mama's back: wipe the kitchen floor, turn the wringer handle to squeeze out more water from the sheets and shirts, refill the woodstove firebox and heat the irons. *If Papa were home,* I thought with a hint of anger, *I wouldn't have to work so hard.*

Escaping at last to my room, I dressed in go-to-town clothes over a film of perspiration from all the work. A tap at my door announced my mother, and I worried immediately: would she tell me I must stay home?

"Molly," she began, "there's a bit of that chicken pie warmed up for you in the kitchen. Make sure you eat before you leave."

In relief, I smiled and said I would.

She twisted to put a hand to her lower back, rubbing. "I'm not much for saying thank you these days," she admitted. "But you're a good help. It's good to have you home." Her face, flushed and hot like mine, creased in a half smile back to me. "Here. The others will have money for some candy, I'm sure. You should too." She pressed a dime into my hand. "Now, behave yourself! I'm going to rest for a few minutes and then I'll be ironing again."

With a quick nod, she vanished into the other bedroom, dodging my grasp.

It was just enough to help me feel that Mama really did love me after all, even if she didn't want to hold me or let me hold on to her. I called "Thank you!" as I tied my quarter for the movie into my handkerchief alongside Mama's dime. I scrambled down the stairs to eat the noon meal she'd left for me and said good-bye to Me-Mere, who also told me to be good.

After all that, I was ready before one o'clock, and I didn't want to wait at my house. So I walked up the hill to the center of the village. I found the car with Jimmy and Ed already in it, at O'Connor's Store, and Katy just slipping into the backseat. I sat beside her, relieved that the boys were both in the front. The top of the Ford Model T, folded down, rested behind us, and I was glad for the sunshine, as a puff of north wind pressed the lingering chill through my coat. I tied my scarf more tightly, for warmth as well as security.

Over the noise of the engine, the wheels on the muddy road, and the wind, I called up to Jimmy: "How long have you been driving?"

I could see the crease by his ear that meant he was grinning, but he didn't turn away from the wheel as he shouted, "Years! But this is the first time I've taken it out of the village. I promised my father I'd split wood all next week!"

Eddie Beck, cheeks flushed with wind and cap pulled down tight, turned toward us girls and warned, "Don't talk to him while he's driving!" His laughter gave away the tease, and we all joined in, grabbing for the handholds as the car bounced on the ruts.

The road was straight, and there were no horses to worry about. With so much noise and wind we gave up on talking, and Katy and I pulled a big wool horse blanket up over our laps. She pointed without trying to talk, and I looked at the houses and farms along the way, amazed at how quickly we passed by each one. The blue sky gave a bright backdrop to the leafless trees between the fields, and a hint of green topped the pastures.

So it seemed no time at all, though it was nearly an hour, to reach St. Johnsbury. Railroad Street, lined with parked cars and full of Saturday shoppers, presented some challenges to Jimmy's driving, but he used brakes and horn alternating, and soon we were parked just beyond the Star Theatre. When I climbed out, my legs wobbled as if the ground still rolled by. I stood next to Katy in the long line of people, with the boys in front of us, as we all waited for the ticket window to open. In town, the sunshine warmed us more, and I opened the buttons of my coat and stood on tiptoe, peering across the heads in front of us to see the bright posters for the double feature.

Inside the theater, I gave up my ticket and stood with the others at the candy stand. My dime from Mama was for a box of candy, and I paid it and pointed to a bright yellow carton of gumdrops. The girl who passed it to me gave it a little shake, to make the candies rattle inside, and it sounded like a lot. Maybe I could save some to take home with me. I saw Katy buy a chocolate bar; so did each of the boys. Eddie asked me if I wanted one. I just said "No, thanks," and we moved farther into the building, to find seats. I expected to sit next to Katy, but Jimmy waved an arm like a gentleman and sent her into the first seat over, and took the next one himself. Eddie stood politely waiting for me to take the third. I shook my head again, "No, thanks," not wanting to be sitting between the two boys. He looked puzzled, so I said quickly, "I'd like to have the aisle seat if you don't mind." With a shrug, he went into the row before me, and I took the last seat in the row with relief. At least nobody was on the other side of me!

I held my box of candy on my lap, wondering when I was supposed to open it. The others were talking and snuggling down into the plush comfort. Eddie turned toward me and started to speak, but the lights flickered and the screen in front of us lit up right away, and people hissed "Shhh!" all around us. Awkwardly, I patted Eddie's arm and whispered "Later!" Then I pushed my folded-up coat between us a bit and curled into as small a space in the seat as I could, trying not to rattle my box of gumdrops.

Even as the pictures flashed on the big, high screen, sitting with so many people distracted me at first. The air felt damp and thick with people smells, sweat and wet wool and a hint of barnyard too. From the seat to my right, I caught a whiff of a low fruity smell that must, I realized, be hair pomade from Eddie's hair.

A huge roaring lion and crackle of blurred sound tore my attention back to the screen, where a newsreel opened, showing crowds of people waiting for handouts in the city. The Depression. I knew about it, but it seemed far away. In Waterford we raised our vegetables and chickens or traded for them just the same as before now. And the dam, as well as the Fairbanks Mill in St. Johnsbury, provided work for men who didn't go to the woods or farm. I watched the grainy dark newsreel and listened to the rough news voice talking loudly.

Then, with a curl of music from the loudspeakers and cheers from around us, the Mickey Mouse cartoon began, called *Steamboat Willie,* silly and lively and funny. I laughed with the crowd, and sucked carefully on my first gumdrop. I couldn't see the color, but the taste was thick and orangey.

When the feature film started, Katy and I swapped dismayed glances across the boys. Marching music, men in uniforms and helmets, outside a school. And a schoolmaster telling the schoolboys they were supposed to fight, fight, fight like men for their fatherland. I could see how the Germans became so dangerous. Then the movie grew darker, with soldiers, guns, and cannons, and one of the soldiers went blind from the shell fire and staggered right into where a machine gun was shooting. It was horrible.

The boys shouted at each success, and in the balcony up over our heads, some people banged their feet when the cannons fired. When Katy stood up and squeezed in front of Jimmy and Eddie, taking my arm and gesturing toward the hallway, I was relieved. We lingered in the powder room, wondering how long it would all last. And when we slipped back into our seats, it seemed like there weren't as many people around us as before, but it might just have been the quiet, as more and more people in the movie got wounded. I felt sick, thinking about what the Great War had really been like.

At least without a romance on the screen, I didn't have to worry about Eddie having ideas about a date or something. I couldn't imagine what it would be like to kiss someone like that, with his red cheeks and wide, damp eyes. Sitting so close, I could smell the pomade again on his hair, a peachy scent, on top of a faint male smell of sweat and skin. I couldn't help thinking how different he was from Henry's cool and quiet outside.

When the film ended and the lights came up, Eddie turned toward me and asked, "What did you think of it?"

I said the first thing that came to mind: "I hate war!"

He nodded, his cheeks still flushed with color, this time from the drama instead of the wind. "That's what you're supposed to feel, that's what this is all about. So we won't have another one, ever." He patted my shoulder and said, "You're a smart girl, Molly. Not everybody catches on to that when they watch this stuff." I blushed.

Pushing us all in front of him, Jimmy talked in a loud voice about what he'd seen. "The best country wins," he repeated from the movie's ending. "America! The Kaiser should have never started that war. And did you see how useless those Frenchies were? A hundred percent Americans, that's what it took to back the Kaiser down. A hundred percent!"

I thought about asking him where those Americans came from before Paul Revere got them all fighting against England. Katy and I were Americans, too! But a small tight shake of Katy's head stopped me from saying it, and I just listened. Mostly the men and boys were talking as we left the theater, and the women were quiet. I guess some of the girls must have felt like I did.

Some of the kids waited outside for rides, and I heard them talking about the next movie coming: a Buck Jones Western called *The Lone Rider*. I shivered, thinking that maybe a war movie wasn't so bad compared to cowboys and Indians. What would Me-Mere say about movies like that? Something angry rose up in me, although I pushed it down again. *It's just boys and girls in town*, I told myself. *Smile and be nice.*

Across the street, a man in a truck watched everyone coming out of the theater. His wide black hat shadowed his face, but I could tell he was looking at us. I nudged Katy and whispered, "The dam boss?"

She poked Jimmy, who twisted his mouth sideways and hissed at Eddie, "He's watching!"

Eddie shrugged, hands in pockets. "I worked my fifty-eight hours. It's not me he's checking up on."

Still, I shivered a moment. The dam boss with his mean look gave me the creeps.

We walked around the corner and climbed back into the car, boys in front, girls in back again. And while the boys got the Ford started, Katy said, "At

least we got out of Waterford for a whole afternoon!"

I wasn't sure that was the greatest thing. But I
forced a smile and said, "Next time, Greta Garbo
instead!"

"Oh, you are bad!" she scolded, grinning.

There was still plenty of daylight left when we
drove back into Waterford. Still, I knew it must be
nearly suppertime, and I scrambled gladly out of the
car when it pulled up by the store. Eddie and Jimmy
climbed out, too, and Jimmy leaned close to Katy,
whispering something to her. Eddie stood next to me,
cheeks red as ever, wiping his eyes from the wind on
a large white handkerchief.

"Thanks," I called over to Jimmy, who waved
and kept talking to my friend. To Eddie I said, "I'm
glad you don't like war either."

"Good enough," he answered. "So, do you, um,
do you want to go to the movies again someday?"

Uh-oh. That did sound like a date. I fumbled
with what I wanted to say, and finally burst out with,
"Well, if Katy is going too, maybe . . ."

He nodded, and I felt like I'd said the right thing
after all. And with a wave at Katy, I started home.

High overhead a hawk circled, eyeing the river
and the fields beyond the houses. Unexpectedly, the

voice I knew was Gratia suddenly said, in an older sister tone, "Too bad Henry Laporte doesn't go to the movies."

I brushed irritably at my left ear, whispered "Cut it out!" and opened the kitchen door, scuffing my feet clean as I entered.

"Well?" said Me-Mere, getting up from the kitchen table to look directly into my face. She smiled at what she saw but didn't ask more than, "So, you had a good time? Are you ready to set the table?"

"Yes." And with some relief, I walked back into being a granddaughter, daughter, and kitchen helper, letting the outside world and its questions fall aside. That is, if Gratia would only let things be!

·❖·

Sunday morning it rained again. There was no church
service, so I helped Mama knead a batch of graham
bread, then pulled on boots and the musty-smelling
mackinaw and slipped outside. The rain wasn't so
bad. I could walk to the river, on the path by the
house. It was a relief to be alone, even with the roar
of the river. The water splashed and lapped at the tops
of the rocky banks, and I didn't dare go close. The
ground shivered underfoot, soft and sodden with so
much rain. Squinting through the mist of raindrops,
I searched for logs in the torrent, but saw only one
bobbing and swirling. The drive must be well downriver, then. I imagined Papa out in the rain also and

wondered when the wanagan had passed through town. Perhaps while I was in school. I should ask Katy; at the store, everyone would know the details.

If Gratia hadn't drowned, she'd be twenty-one.

Some marsh-marigold stems and leaves flared deep green in a hollow to one side of where I stood. Moving to get a closer look at them, looking for the bright yellow buds and flowers, I nearly tripped over a cedar stake in the soft ground. About four feet high, it had numbers marked on the flat side. Another one stood at the far side of the hollow.

Walking over to the second one, I discovered a third. And more. They seemed to outline an area of the low ground. I could make no sense of the numbers, but the direction was clear: toward my house. Curious, I wandered along the route, counting them. Twelve, fifteen—the route crossed the river road just uphill of our house and continued east, roughly parallel to the river itself but perhaps a quarter mile from the main channel.

Another set of numbers came to me as I stood wondering: the new baby. It would be born in September, so it would be nearly sixteen and a half years younger than I was. So when I was twenty-one myself, as Gratia would have been today, the new little boy or girl would be almost five years old. And Gratia had been five years old when she drowned. I tugged at the figures, sensing some kind of pattern.

Looking for a pattern suddenly made me see the cedar stakes differently. Could they be surveyor stakes?

I turned abruptly for home and, after dropping boots and coat by the kitchen door, went looking for my grandmother. She was in her bedroom, the one behind the kitchen. The door stood half open, so I rapped on the door frame and stuck my head around, to see her sitting by the window. She cocked her head to one side and peered at me brightly. "Well? What is it?"

"Me-Mere," I said slowly, "when the dam is finished, the lake will grow. Is that so?"

"That is so," she agreed. "Although we'll still hear the voice of the Long River beyond the ends of the lake. There will be a waterfall at the dam, which will have a very loud voice." She paused. "And so, granddaughter?"

I hesitated, twisting a strand of my hair, and she patted my hand away from it, clucking her tongue at the habit. "Well," I said, "what I wonder is, how big will the lake grow to be?"

"Ah." She cocked her head the other way, then stood and turned to the window. "It will grow to be a little higher on this slope than the house is now. There is a plan to make the lake very wide, and eight miles long."

The end of her amazing sentence hung between us, until finally I broke forth: "Then the water will cover our house?"

"Oh, no," she replied reassuringly. "The lake won't be that deep here. But it will cover where our house has stood, yes. Change comes to everyone, Molly."

"I don't understand! Will we move our house?"

"No." She sat again in the chair, fingers rubbing through her blouse at the old necklace she wore hidden beneath it. "No, the power company will knock it down into the foundation, perhaps burning the boards, or perhaps someone will carry the boards away." She looked into my face and waited.

Fear and anger, one after the other, swept into me. "Why didn't you tell me—or Mama or Papa, why didn't they? I'm not a child—you should have told me!" I couldn't help yelling, and I shouted again, "Somebody should have told me!"

"Shhh!" Out of her chair she scrambled, to close the door of her room. "Your mother is asleep!" She faced me, glaring. "You certainly sound like a child right now, don't you?"

Furious, I glared back.

She spat out more explanation: "Your mother and father wanted you to finish the school year before they told you. In September," she announced firmly, "we are all moving up the hill, into the village. Your father has signed the papers for the other house." Again she stopped, and I struggled, trying to catch up with the way my world was tilting.

"Which other house?" I demanded, trying not to shout.

"The house across from the school, where Mrs. Wells lives. She's going down to Connecticut to live with her son, and she's sold your father the house." And in a final pronouncement, she told me, "It will be a good time to brush out everyone's hair to look pretty, you see."

"Actually, what I see," I said slowly and angrily, "is that nobody thinks I need to know anything around here. And I am not moving to Mrs. Wells's house. I am not leaving our house. I am staying here!"

Me-Mere leaned forward, pushing her face toward mine and dropping her voice to a near whisper. "Granddaughter, if you want to be a child about this, stamp your foot and run to your room. And if you want to show me you're not a child, button your lip and set the table for supper!"

Abruptly, she tapped the top of my head with

142

one fingertip, then pressed past me to her chair and looked out the window again, not at me.

I won't! That's all I wanted to say, to shout, to stamp both feet and bang doors and more. Caught in my grandmother's trap, I quivered with anger and stood silent, staring beyond her toward where I'd seen the surveyors' stakes and their nasty numbers. I wanted to be a river of rage and fill my grandmother's room.

Slowly, instead, I froze the fury inside myself. As if I could make ice, I froze it into place and turned away from Me-Mere and walked, without stamping, out of her room, deliberately closing the door behind me. Fork by fork, I laid out my anger onto the supper table. Mama's place, Mama who didn't think I was old enough to know we would lose our house. Papa's place, no fork, Papa was still on the river. I blamed him for that, too, being away when he should have been here to do something. Me-Mere's place. Grim and silent, I reversed fork and knife, leaving a message on the table to say how wrong this all was.

And my place.

Anguish struck in my stomach. My place. My house. My life.

It hurt so much, and I nursed the block of ice back into place in the center of my chest. Oh, yes, I could tell: It was still April. Nasty, rainy, death-soaked April. Gratia's month. The month of losses. And now, the month of anger.

Going out like a spring lamb, ha! Not my April. Going out like a killing frost and a pile of blackened leaves, that's what it was.

·✦·

I suppose Me-Mere told Mama that I knew about
the house. Supper was a quiet, chilly meal, Mama
still tired, Me-Mere watching me for signs of being
a child instead of an adult—at least, that's what it
felt like—and me so angry I could hardly swallow. I
slept with my anger that night, too, and when a hard
rain began in the middle of the dark hours, I tasted
bitterness. In the gray morning, rain still pounded the
windows, and I heard the roar of the river, the night's
waters making it deeper and louder than ever.

Monday.

My planned afternoon walk in the woods with
Henry Laporte looked uncertain. Who would walk
in cold rain, in leafless woods? Nothing was going

right in my life. Then again, considering that I wasn't sure I wanted to walk with Henry anyway, maybe the rain was a good thing.

I pursed my lips in disgust. Nothing was good. Especially not Monday—the day that Mrs. Willson, Mrs. Simpson, even Mrs. O'Connor, would all bring the wash from the week before, including sometimes their Sunday dresses and their husbands' shirts, as well as tablecloths. My personal nightmares were tablecloths: too big to iron on the ironing board, heavy, and often needing stains taken out and small holes mended.

Slumping and tired already, I entered the steam-filled kitchen with reluctance. Mama had sheets and tablecloths in the wash boiler already; I could smell vinegar in the steam, her special way of loosening stains before adding the soap. Mama was on her own; to my questioning look, she said, "Your grandmother already had breakfast. Yours is on the table."

Under the eye-watering steam of vinegar came a hint of cinnamon, and I found warm cinnamon buns and coffee waiting at my place. I lifted a skeptical eyebrow: Mama and Me-Mere knew I loved cinnamon buns. Well, they wouldn't win me over to their plan so easily. For a wild moment I wondered whether there was a way to stop the dam, stop the river turning to lake, stop the loss of my home.

But Papa had signed the papers on the other house, I thought. Nothing was right.

At least Mama and Me-Mere, who came out of her room again to help as the wash water needed changing, didn't talk much. Once Mama said, "There's a bigger kitchen at the other house." But I ignored her words, and she stopped trying to say more.

Just as we poured off the second wash and moved the clothes into the dry sink for a cold rinse, Mama began to cough, a low rattling cough that sounded like Me-Mere's old-lady cough. She stood back from the sink, laboring for breath between choking gasps. Me-Mere poured hot coffee into a tin mug and brought it over, while I patted Mama's back and asked, fresh anger in me, "Mama, how long have you been coughing like this?"

She waved me aside and sipped at the coffee instead, sinking onto a chair. Me-Mere and I took over with the wet linens. I shot a glance back over my shoulder at my mother: one hand cupped her belly, and with the other she held a handkerchief to her mouth as she coughed longer and harder. "Mama?"

She shook her head, took another sip of hot coffee, and struggled to quiet the cough. "It's nothing," she finally said from behind us. "Just a spring cold."

"I'll make you a tea now," my grandmother announced.

I said without thinking, "I'm walking in the woods with Henry Laporte later on. I could ask him for something, maybe slippery elm bark or cherry?"

"Pshaw," spat my grandmother. "I have what your mother needs! Our family takes care of each other without a boy running to the woods for us."

Stung, I replied, "He's not a boy, he's a man. He's sixteen."

"And so are you, and does that make you a woman?" shot back Me-Mere.

"As a matter of fact, it does."

And that was the end of talking for the morning. Of course, it didn't stop the talking inside me, as I ached with anger and loss, thinking about my home and moving and what I wanted to say to Papa but couldn't because he wasn't there, to Mama but couldn't upset her because she was expecting, to Me-Mere but didn't dare.

Trying to prove I was a woman to Me-Mere's critical gaze, I saw, would not be easy. And probably,

I admitted with a glimmer of bitter humor, probably would not end. Ever.

Soon I realized the rain had let up, and by noon, the sun shone brightly. In the moist heat, a haze hung over the garden. Mama propped open the door from the kitchen to the porch, and I carried tubs of wash out to the lines in the yard, pegging the heavy linens in neat, tight rectangles, trying to pull them tight enough to ease the ironing.

The three of us ate while standing and working, with two more women from the village bringing baskets of soiled work clothes that smelled of barn and field, and we moved endless buckets of water on and off the woodstove.

I kept an eye on the time, and when it was nearly three, I told Mama I needed to wash up and go walking. "I'll iron after supper," I promised her.

"Go." She waved me off. "Go enjoy the sunshine. You've worked hard."

So much work and heat and sharing the effort, I noticed, made an inner heat, too. I wasn't as icily angry now. Just sad, mostly.

Up the road to the village I walked steadily, turned to pass the school and realized I was also passing the house Papa had bought, and I refused to look at it.

My tree where I'd read so many books, how could I leave that? And Me-Mere's gardens, and the river.

Ah, the river. How could I hate it so much and also not want to move so far away from it?

I squinted down toward the brown, foaming waters visible in patches between houses, barns, and stands of trees. *Gratia's river,* I thought. And automatically corrected it: *The Long River. Not Gratia's at all.*

Was this what it meant to be sixteen? Everything was changing. Inside me was just plain Molly losing her home. And my best friend was going to Montpelier for next year's school. And for the first time, I was going to be an older sister.

I began to hope that the walk with Henry Laporte might be different from the changes in the rest of my life after all.

·✦·

Henry Laporte waited for me, where the river road met the farm road to his home. He stood quietly, watching the sky to the south, where four or five large birds wheeled against the cloud-smeared blue afternoon sky. I tried to walk quietly, the way a person should walk in the woods and around wild animals. Still, I could hear the crunch of my own shoes on the road and knew he must hear them, too. When I was close enough to see the details of his neatly buttoned shirt, pocketed wool vest, and clean trousers, he turned his face toward me, eyes wide, and said with a gesture upward, "They see more than we do."

"Are they hawks?" I stopped a few feet from him and counted: five.

"No. Turkey buzzards. A family of them."

"How can you tell?"

"Look at the narrow heads." He directed with a half wave of one hand. "And the rough tips to the wings, like feathers that don't line up quite with the others. And the size of the circles, too," he added.

Buzzards. There were buzzards in all the Western stories. "Are they looking at something that's dying?" I ventured.

He looked at me with some surprise. "Good question. Probably it's something already dead, though, maybe with people working too close to it for the birds to drop down yet."

"Like?"

"Like a dead calf sometimes, or maybe something crushed on the roadway. They're circling over the dam site. Where the teams are pulling."

"Oh."

A kind of quiet seeped from Henry into the day. Time slowed. For a few minutes we stood watching the birds circle, and no wagons, no trucks, no people came into the part of the road where we waited. Finally I asked, "Which way are we walking?"

"This way." Henry waved down the farm road. "We'll go up on the ridge. We'll cross a stretch of willows on the way. And I'll show you where to see the whole valley."

"Okay."

The farm road, rutted and puddled, had a narrow ridge down the center that stood higher than the wet mud. Clumps of short brown grass and bits of green weeds crouched on it. We stepped along this narrow way, with Henry in front, me following a few feet behind. It was an awkward way to walk because we couldn't see each other's faces or talk. Henry stopped a moment, turning, to say, "Just past the house it changes to a wide trail. Then we'll talk again."

I nodded, and watched around his shoulders for a first look at the farmhouse where he lived. His mother should be home, I guessed. His father, like mine, rode the river with the spring logs. I knew he had two older brothers. And as the house came into view, I looked for signs of who was there.

A drift of wood smoke rose from the chimney. Shabby white boards in need of paint gave the front of the long farmhouse a sad look. No clothes hung on the double clothesline near the kitchen door, and on the ruts that led toward the barn I saw a farm truck, empty. Through a half-open barn door came the sound of a few cows and something clanking.

"Shhh," Henry cautioned over his shoulder. "My brother's milking. Let's not disturb him."

He didn't want his brother to see us. I understood; it was like not wanting Mama and Me-Mere to make assumptions about the walk. I quieted my feet again and murmured, "Okay." And quickly we passed the house, its curtained windows quiet and dark. The kitchen must look out to the rear, I decided. By this time of day, Henry's mother, like mine, must be working at the woodstove, starting supper.

The rutted farm road curved toward the barn. We left it, moving onto a gently worn trail that crossed in front of the house and quickly entered the low bare woods, winding uphill immediately. It did indeed widen, and I caught up with Henry and walked next to him, my jacketed arm swinging just a few inches from his shirtsleeve. His hands were deep in his pockets, and he didn't turn to look at me but made room on the trail. I watched his gaze rise up along the dark tree trunks, over the thickets of brush, and again toward the sky, although I saw he shot little glances at the ground often.

Walking so close, I could smell the woods on him as well as around us: a sweet hint of sawdust mixed with balsam fir and the dampness of wet bark and stone. And there came a tang of wood smoke from his damp vest. Slanted rays of afternoon sun broke through and lit the bare branches. Willing myself to look harder, to see more, I noticed swollen tips on most of the branches. Dark like old blood, they must be buds.

"Why aren't they green?" I wondered aloud.

"Mmm. Another good question. They come up dark, and see, the deer won't eat as many of them if they look the same as the branches. But when there's enough warmth and sun, the leaves burst out of them all at once. If the deer haven't eaten them, see?"

I did. Eyeing the brush more closely, I said, "There aren't any deer up here with us though, are there?"

In answer, Henry stopped and pointed down at the soil by my feet. "One's been here just a few minutes ago," he murmured. "A little mama, hungry, swollen up and almost ready for her fawns."

I knelt, staring at the pair of curved marks on the ground. "How do you know?"

Henry squatted on his heels and, holding a stick, pointed at the edges of the track. "Sharp edges, even though the mud is soft enough to collapse again quickly. So it's a new track. And it's too big to be a baby, and it's deep, so the deer is heavy. And if it were a buck instead, with a track this deep you'd see the points from the other toes. It's a very heavy doe.

And hungry, she has to be hungry, to be walking the trail this late."

So he put the pieces together, in that calm voice, and I felt stroked with quiet. I didn't want to look right in his face, but I angled sideways to glance, and I liked the familiar shapes, cheekbones that reminded me of my father's, though the mouth, I thought, was nothing like the ones in my own family. I caught another scent, the scent of warm human breath, and pulled back from such strangeness, standing slowly up.

"That's neat," I told him. He stood up, too. "Thank you." I meant it.

Nodding, he started forward again. In a moment he pointed to a triplet of dark green leaves and a nearly hidden, dark red-tipped bud at the center. New life was pressing upward from the dead winter ground.

More quickly than I expected, we reached a ridge near the top of the hill. I followed on the narrower path, and all at once the valley lay in front of us, misty and damp. Dark wet roofs of houses stood along the roads. The red jacket of a child rose up and down on a swing at the school yard. I heard a dog bark and listened hard to isolate the soft distant swish of the river. A silver line of railroad tracks wove west, away from the scar of the dam work site.

"The train comes out in the morning, with some of the men and supplies," Henry said, watching me. "It goes back to St. Johnsbury about five. Soon enough."

From here I could also see the housing for the workers: long dormitories and rows of cabins for the hundreds of workers, some French Canadian, some local, some Irish even. And there was a truck, smoke pluming as it growled over a bank of gravel near the river.

"We don't see that many of the men in town," I marveled.

"Mmm. They go to St. Johnsbury on the train instead," he agreed. "More stores. More people. More things to do. Movie theaters and such."

By the drop of his voice, I could tell he didn't think much of that. I spoke up defensively: "Movies are fun."

"I guess," came the unenthusiastic reply.

So different, I mused. Funny how he seemed a little familiar, a little like people I knew but so different from my friends. I searched for something else to say. "Do you come up here a lot?"

"Not really. Maybe now and then."

The silence between us grew again. Just as I thought I'd need to cut the silence with something, anything, stupid or not, a flash of movement in the field below caught my eye. "Look! It's a fox, isn't it?" And though I spoke in a low voice, the creature below seemed to hear me, looking up for a moment, then running in a zigzag across the brown, muddy pasture. "What's it doing?" I demanded urgently. "It's jumping!"

"Caught something." I could hear Henry's smile. "Mouse or maybe a chipmunk. Everything's hungry this time of year." I looked quickly at him, as his hands rustled in his vest pockets. Out came two apples, winter wrinkled but clean and soft and unexpectedly fragrant.

I took one, and the two of us eased back into a kinder sort of quiet, looking out, while chewing the soft warm fruit. "Thanks."

This time I knew he'd just nod, and it made me smile to realize I already knew something more about this boy. This man. Oh, that sounded old. Just . . . just Henry.

I expected his hand brushing against mine, the way Eddie had touched my arm at the movie theater. But he didn't reach out again after giving me the apple, and mostly I was relieved. Mostly.

After a bit, we stood up and walked down the slope on a different trail, one that dipped into a small swamp where Henry led the way from stone to tree trunk and finally to a dry, firm trail again. Twice within the swamp he stopped and showed me large gray-barked trees that stood on their own in the soggy ground: black ash, the basket tree. I could see a hint of purple color to the twigs and asked why.

"Those are the buds, not the twigs," Henry explained. "Tree flowers come before the leaves do."

As we climbed lower, the ground firmed, then settled toward a pond, where among last year's cattails a chorus of peepfrogs sang. A duck suddenly flapped up into the air, quacking. Henry gestured, and we moved away to let the duck settle. He nodded toward a cluster of nearby bushes whose branch tips glowed a soft yellow in the gentle, late afternoon light.

"Basket willow," I guessed aloud, and his nod and smile made me glow.

The trail wound around until it came out on the river road, not the Laporte farm road. I realized this must be about where I'd been running into Henry recently. So he'd been out in the willow swamp, or up on the ridge on those other days, I decided. That was another thing I knew about him now.

We stood facing each other at the side of the road, a foot apart, and after a moment, he nodded one more time. "Your mother and grandmother probably want you home for supper," he pointed out. "If you walk pretty quickly, you'll be there in time."

"We don't eat until six," I said reflexively.

"I know," he said. "I mean, I've seen the lights change at your house about that time, when I walk home from the other side of the valley."

Focused on what that might mean, I guessed again: "From where the black ash trees are?"

"Mmm. Not exactly. From fishing, mostly." He must have seen the surprise in my face, for he continued: "In the winter I help with morning chores and anything in the fields or the barn, but my brothers are around enough so I can go out to the woods or the river in the afternoons most days. At least when we're not sugaring. And then maybe half the time I'm coming home through the village that way, and I stop at the store to pick up empty baskets that go back to my mother. From the bread she bakes."

Oh. Well, that explained how he'd seen our house so much. Anyone who fished along the river would pass near us, and of course we were pretty near the store. So Henry knew something about me too.

"And it's almost six now," he added with a half smile.

"Well, I better go then," I said. I wasn't sure how I was supposed to say good-bye.

Henry seemed more sure: "I'll see you again," he said with a tilt of his face, a widening of his dark eyes. "When you want to see more of the woods as it changes."

"All right."

I walked as quickly as I could, hearing my shoes slap and crunch against the road. When, after a few minutes, I turned to look back, I could see Henry partway down the farm road, also hurrying. Coincidentally, he half turned at that moment and looked my way, and raised one arm to wave.

I waved back, then raced home, to where the evening lamps glowed and the aroma of fragrant supper mingled with the thick scent of clean, damp sheets that had just been taken into the kitchen.

Me-Mere brushed a quick hand over my damp hair, and Mama asked whether I was hungry while she ladled beef stew into a plate. It surprised me that they didn't ask me right away about my walk with Henry, although I saw them exchange glances when they thought I wasn't looking up from my supper. I said casually, "It was a nice day for walking in the woods. I saw some signs of spring."

"Oh, yes?" My mother smiled gently and turned to Me-Mere. "You'll be wanting to walk there soon, for the leeks and the fiddlehead ferns, won't you?"

"Not yet," my grandmother said. She added casually, "Did your young man show you any new plants?"

I swallowed too quickly and reached for a glass of cold water to wash down the hot mouthful. "He's not my young man, Me-Mere. He's just Henry Laporte, you know him. I went to see where he finds the black ash up there, that's all."

I gave each of my grinning relatives a scowl, but I felt too good to hold the cross face, and smiled again, repeating, "We just walked."

They nodded, and pointedly I ignored them while I finished my supper. But I didn't mind the teasing really. In my mind's eye I saw the view from the ridge and a sideways view of Henry, not quite looking at me, but listening and watching, so that I mattered as much as a bird or a fox whose life he watched from his hill.

That was a good thing, to matter that much, I felt. But it didn't make Henry "my young man," and I wasn't "his young woman" either. It was just, I repeated to myself, just a walk with somebody different, and nice.

As I settled to a cup of tea with my supper and my mother and grandmother, the calendar on the wall caught my eye. Only one more day of April. Maybe the better days of May, for me, had already started. I would have to tell Katy all about it.

Well, maybe not all. I smiled.

SUMMER

·✦·

·✹·

Papa was home.

I lay in bed in the early light of a June morning, listening to the *cheeri-oh, cheeri-oh* of robins outside my window and knowing that everything was all right now. For Papa had been home since Friday night, and in just a day and a half, life had become simple again. Yesterday, a hot sunny June Saturday, Papa had turned the vegetable garden and planted the beans, corn, squashes. By afternoon he was fixing things: the shelf in the mudroom, a rack for airing sheets, the sagging far end of the clothesline.

Mama made custard pies. Me-Mere disappeared for part of the afternoon, returning with a basket of fiddlehead fern tops, a lush green for supper. And for the first time in weeks, there was time for me to sit with Katy by the river, time for us to talk about all that May had brought.

I rolled over and pressed my face into the pillow, escaping the sunshine for a moment, thinking about what Katy had told me:

"There's a dance at the Pavilion in West Barnet, a start-the-summer party. It's in two weeks. Jimmy says we could all go together, all four of us, a double date. Except"—she adapted to the doubt in my face—"you and Eddie don't have to be a date really, just come along with Jimmy and me so my father won't say no. Anyway, half the parents in the village will probably be there," she added dismissively. "You'll come, Molly, won't you?"

For a moment the mischief of the Irish vanished, and Katy had simply pleaded. How could I say no? *She's my best friend,* I repeated to myself now, *and we only have this summer. I have to go with her.*

Robin sounds persisted just under my window. And the light was so bright. Rolling back over, I kicked off the coverlet and padded to the window. Yes, the birds were repairing last year's nest in the apple tree. The brighter one bounced on a branch tip, his brown and orange feathers ruffled, and he sang a challenge into the day. Then he flew off. I stayed very still, and a moment later the mother robin arrived, mouth full of straw. She reminded me of my own mother, clothespins pursed in her lips, pegging sheets and shirts onto the line.

Katy's sweet on Jimmy, I thought.

Though I wasn't sweet on Eddie in any sense, I liked it that he'd asked Jimmy to ask Katy to ask me to come to the dance.

I heard the floor creak, and turned to see Me-Mere at the doorway to my room. She held a finger up for quiet, and whispered, "Come downstairs with me—the coffee's hot, and I'll brush your hair."

I smiled. My grandmother loved to brush hair and braid it, but she hadn't brushed mine in a long time. Surely this was another sign of Papa being home: everyone could slip back to old ways, be comfortable, be safe.

Me-Mere vanished down the stairs, and I pulled on my clothes: blouse, sweater, corduroy skirt, knee-high socks. Though it was Sunday, there would be no church service in the village; the minister did not ride over from East St. Johnsbury in the summer months. More likely, someone might come calling at mid-morning, to pay a visit.

In the kitchen the luxury of a day off from the washing made the summer morning even better. After my grandmother gave my hair a hundred strokes of the hairbrush and braided the length of it—a single braid wound around into a loop, a woman's braid, not an Abenaki child's pair of them—Me-Mere and I sat at the table with sweet coffee made pale with cream, each listening to the quiet inside the house and the racket of birdsong outside.

Finally my grandmother stretched and stood. "Cinnamon rolls," she proposed. "The dough is ready. Help me make the snails."

The old nickname from childhood made me grin. We'd finger the bits of dough into "snakes," dip them in milk, then in cinnamon sugar, and curl them into "snails" that would rise into perfect swirled rolls. "Good," I answered. "But we'd better be quick!" A set of creaks and soft thumps over our heads said Mama and Papa would soon join us in the kitchen.

It was a perfect summer Sunday morning.

When, after breakfast, the knock at the front door came, I had my arms in the dishpan, and Mama, coughing a little, moved toward the front room. Papa and I exchanged glances: who would come to the closed front door when the kitchen door stood wide open, ready for neighbors? After a moment, Papa followed Mama, and I heard a man talking with them, and Mama inviting the visitor to step in for coffee.

I lugged the pan of dishwater out the kitchen door, poured it out onto the peonies growing thick in a clump by the steps, and hurried back in.

But the guest hadn't come back to the kitchen with Papa and Mama after all.

"Who was it?" I asked Mama. She held a hand to her mouth as she coughed again, unable to answer right away, and reached with the other hand for her coffee cup.

Papa replied instead. "It's Mr. Wilkins, the boss from the dam site. He's looking for more help for the summer."

I saw the possibilities right away. "Will you take the work, Papa? You could stay home all summer, not go back to the woods until the snow!" That would be a very good thing for taking care of Mama, if she needed it. I realized I didn't know enough about her condition; when would she need to slow down? Mounds of future wash huddled in my thoughts, and I dreaded the idea that I might have to do more of Mama's work than I was already doing. It would help if Papa were home, I decided. And besides, the thought of moving from one house to the other swept back over me, and I thought bitterly, Papa should do the packing; it was Papa who'd signed the papers to see our house get flooded over.

My father nodded. "I told him I'd start tomorrow."

I turned back to the empty dishpan, wiping it dry and trying to keep the relief off my face.

"And I'll keep an eye on all the young men," my father teased. "So they won't think they can come courting my young lady daughter!"

"Oh!" With everyone smiling, I realized I shouldn't miss the chance to mention the dance. "Papa, speaking of young men—there's a dance the Grange is putting on, in West Barnet. Katy asked me to go with her. It's not a date, it's just a group of us going together, if that would be all right."

My father frowned: "Who's in this group?" Out of the corner of my gaze I watched my mother and grandmother holding still and listening, too. I explained carefully.

"Well, Katy, of course, and Jimmy Johnson and Eddie Beck. They both work at the dam now, Papa; they're hard workers."

A look flew between my parents as Papa hesitated. He said at last, "You'll all stay together?"

"We will," I promised. "And there'll be other people from Waterford there too, Papa. It's the Grange, you know."

Repeating the part about the Grange tipped the

balance, making my grandmother nod from her chair. As my father began to agree, I jumped to kiss his cheek and say "Thank you, thank you!" He patted my shoulder and warned, "I'll be working with those boys next week. If they're not good ones, I'll know, and I'll change my mind!"

"You won't have to change your mind," I assured him. In the sunny moment, even my mother smiled.

There was just time to make the beds before I slipped out of the humming house to walk up to the village. No church, and short store hours, too; Katy might be able to walk along the river, if she wasn't cooking with her mother.

As I walked up the steps of the store, I heard laughter and a jumble of voices. Darn. Sure enough, the place bustled with slicing, wrapping, talking. I stood just inside the door, said hello, and watched Katy weigh out four pounds of sugar. She glanced at the clock in the corner and threw me a quick wave: "About four o'clock?"

Waving back, I agreed, and ducked back out onto the front porch. Now what? Four hours, more or less, before Katy would be free to come out. Without thinking about it, I wandered toward the covered bridge, listening to the river and its cleaner summer sound. At the center of the bridge, I stopped and peered through the triangular gap at the water below. No longer muddy, it sparkled, a light tea color from the mountain soils, little bits of froth along the edges. Though the bridge roof shaded me, the sun was hot and strong. I sniffed the water scent, so different from the spring version. I could feel late afternoon swimming holes in memory and anticipation. Carefully, I let myself listen for Gratia in the summer waters, but there was no voice, no sense of her. Maybe she didn't call from such safe waters.

Still, someone was calling my name. Eddie—coming into the bridge from the far side, fishing rod on his shoulder, bucket in the other hand.

He rushed through the "How you doing?" parts and burst out with, "Did Katy give you the message? Can you come to the dance?"

I hesitated. "I can come, but, well, it's not a date, okay?" Quickly, so he wouldn't be hurt, I added a "white lie": "My parents don't want me dating yet, you know?"

It worked. He grinned. "I know. Mine neither. But I'm really glad you're coming." He glanced into his bucket, where five or six fish lay, bright colors vanished into muted silver sheen. "Gotta go. But I'm really, really glad, you know?"

I blushed and looked down. "Yeah," I murmured, and he laughed and left the bridge, hurrying through the village and turning north, along the empty river road.

No Katy, Eddie gone, no Gratia. Though my pulse raced from talking with Eddie, the quiet of the sunny afternoon wrapped around me. I walked the rest of the way over the bridge away from the store, to pick a handful of daisies and early buttercups. Then, back through the cool shaded tunnel of the bridge, I headed home to put my flowers in water and find a book to read until four. I slipped quietly past the gardens, where my grandmother weeded with her back toward me, and entered the still house. Where were my parents? Maybe they were outside, too. After setting my flowers in a short blue vase, I tiptoed upstairs.

Reading *Gulliver's Travels* for the second time still made me uncomfortable, especially the part where the Lilliputians were tying up the sleeping hero, so after a few chapters I closed my eyes and let my head down onto my arms, the fresh clean scent of the bedcover adding itself to the summer fragrance in the room. Drifting, I must have eased into a dream, for suddenly Gratia was talking to me. "So you're going to the dance and Eddie is going to want to dance with you," she warned. "Hold your hand, too. Maybe try to kiss you. I can't talk to you when you're doing all that stuff."

"Good," I replied to the stern little five-year-old glaring at me in the dream. "You're just a little girl. You don't understand."

"I understand about Henry," she poked back at me. "You're sweet on him, like Eddie's sweet on you. I can tell."

"None of your business," I retorted. "Mind your own dumb old business anyway!"

"I hate you!" Gratia's voice rose. "I hate you, I hate you! Go ahead, kiss some stupid boy. I won't even watch!"

"Good!"

Saying "Good!" out loud woke me suddenly, lost for a moment in the bedroom. Good? Was it good to tell Gratia to get out of my way? I shivered. I didn't want her gone, didn't want her dead.

Shaking my head, I realized: *She's already dead. She's a little girl. She won't understand what it's like to grow up.*

"But I have to keep growing up," I whispered into the room. Nothing answered — not Gratia, and not any spirit or person. So I tugged at my coiled braid and took it all apart, letting my hair fall loose behind me, and stared into the narrow looking glass, wondering: if I stopped hearing Gratia's voice, would I be more normal after all? Maybe that was the safest way to be.

Katy didn't get away from the store after all on Sunday, so I had a quiet evening. Not talking about Henry much with her somehow made me quiet all the way through, as I thought about the walk, the trees, the animals, and what had happened—and hadn't.

Monday was wash day, for all the village and especially for my mother and grandmother and me. Tuesday was ironing. Thank goodness, I am terrible with the iron—so my mother and Me-Mere set me free from ironing at midafternoon and sent me with their list to the store. Katy wasn't there. I told her mother I'd come back around four if I could. I took home the canning rubbers and paraffin and matches

I'd been told to fetch, and walked back up the hill to the little library across from the wide white inn.

The librarian, Miss Gagnon, sat behind the wide wooden desk piled with books being returned or asked about. Seeing her, tidy in a neat wool suit despite the summer air, with her white hair carefully pinned up above her forehead, I relaxed. Miss Gagnon had always been there, always would. At least, on Tuesday and Thursday afternoons she would.

"Miss Molly," she chirped with a bright nod, and spun on her chair to rummage in a pile of books behind the desk. "I have something for you, and isn't it just perfect that you're here?" She beamed, and handed me a book in a bright wrapper.

I turned it curiously: The front showed a stylish girl about my own age, with cropped blond hair, wearing one of the new cloche hats and a daringly short skirt that barely covered her knees. *The Secret of the Old Clock,* I read aloud.

"It's the very newest mystery, about a young woman named Nancy Drew," Miss Gagnon enthused. "We have an entire set, three adventures. I thought you might like to be the very first borrower of this one."

An honor! Miss Gagnon marked the names of borrowers on the card for each book, and she pointed to them with great pride: the town leaders who read

Les Miserables, for instance, and the boys and men taking home *Robinson Crusoe.*

Gently I thumbed the pages of the book. Not much more than two hundred pages — I could read it this week, maybe. Before the dance.

Thinking about the dance made me itchy again, unwilling to stay still. I told Miss Gagnon thanks, and said I'd take the book home; she filled out the card in her lovely sloped penmanship and wrapped the book in a sheet of newspaper for me to carry.

So once more I slipped quietly back into my own house, set the book by my bed, and, determined to at least take a longer walk, tiptoed down the front stairs and edged out through the front door, avoiding the kitchen where the irons surely still hissed. The scent of hot fabric assured me of that.

Back on the road, the afternoon sun heated my face and I squinted as I walked west, along the road that would pass Henry Laporte's farm road and eventually would rise over the mountain to St. Johnsbury. But I wouldn't walk that far. Instead, why not take the other side road, the one toward the dam site, to see what all the men were working on? Of course, I'd need to stay in the trees, where Papa wouldn't catch sight of me! I grinned, knowing what trouble I'd be in if Papa ever thought I'd been to where the big crew of men labored.

The road to the dam left the main road just beyond the Laporte farm road. Deeply rutted, soft and wet, the double wheel beds were hard to walk in. I tried to balance on the center ridge, a bit drier underfoot, and listened to the rumble of machinery ahead. The train? No, that would be later, at the end of the workday. Cranes and earth-moving tractors and trucks, I decided. The ground shook and the air hung much too full of low rumbling around me.

As I got farther from the main road, and closer to the river, I could see more sky through the trees to either side. Any moment the roadway would open out into cleared space. I edged off the road and into the trees, lifting my skirts a bit so they wouldn't catch on twigs and thorns. Then the ground cover changed away from scrubby stems to soft green ferns, easier to pass through. I found a faint line of crushed grass that I guess was from the deer passing through, so I followed it to a clump of poplars, where I stood partly behind a large thick trunk, peering down into the river plain.

Enormous stone and cement wings of the dam towered over the plain. Around them, at least a dozen vehicles moved, mostly slowly, loaded or tugging or pushing. I saw a group of men in work caps leaning against a platform, waiting for a crane to lower its swinging steel beam in front of them. Up on top of the closer wing, more men hammered on a roof of a building that sat high up, probably for some future controller to turn levers and watch the waters.

In the shadow of such size and the hundreds of men, in clusters of work, the river itself looked small and thin. How long would it take, once the dam closed, for the river waters to rise into a lake? To rise over our house?

Resentment soured my stomach. Why hadn't anyone told me sooner that our house would be taken away by the new lake? I wondered: *When the Long River is caught like this, will it rage? Will floods pound at the dam?*

I shivered. I strained into the busy air to listen for Gratia's voice under or over it, but she seemed silent. What dark river shadow did her spirit cling to? Her body, I knew, lay in the village cemetery. But knowing her voice so well, I knew my grandmother's talk of spirits must be so. Something of Gratia moved as easily as water through me.

Why hadn't I brought something to look through, to see which men were doing what? A telescope, or opera glasses even, like the ones in the front room in the china cupboard. From here, I couldn't tell which man was my father, or even where the boys from school were working. So much activity, but without names and faces, so that after a little while it all seemed dull. I turned slowly, not wanting to attract any attention from below, and eased back into the fern bed. I wasn't quite on the deer trail this time, but walked through the tallest ferns, some of them nearly reaching my waist although the summer was still early.

A faint scent reached me even before my feet felt the difference, the thinning, the opening in the ferns. I pulled up short just in time, for at my feet was a fawn lying in the ferns.

Its wide, wet eyes gazed at me, thick black nostrils flaring. A flicker of muscle under the beautiful brown and white pelt told me of its fear, in spite of its stillness. Gently I knelt, coming down to its height, crooning softly: "It's all right, little one. I won't hurt you."

It didn't understand. I saw another ripple of fear twitch through its back. I wanted to reassure it, and reached a hand to lightly touch the warm side of its neck. "Shhh," I whispered. "Shhh, baby. There, there."

The scent was a mix of creature and warmth,

and heat under my hand pulsed with such a rapid heartbeat. I smoothed the thick hair down toward its back.

"Better not touch it more," came a quiet voice from behind me, and I fell over from my kneeling position as I tried to whip around to see who it was.

"Henry! What are you doing here?"

"Saw you," he replied quietly. "Wanted to be sure you didn't lose your way."

"In this bitty bit of trees?" I sniffed, pulling back up to stand, awkwardly smoothing my skirt.

"Slowly," he cautioned. "It's afraid of us."

He was right: my louder voice and quick movement made the fawn shiver. I bent to stroke it again, thinking I could pick it up to comfort it. It was only the size of a large dog; it wouldn't be too heavy.

"Better not," Henry repeated. "If the mother smells your smell on the baby, she might abandon it."

I knew he was right. My father had always told me that, about baby birds in the spring, and baby raccoons. Deer would act the same way.

Reluctantly, I pulled away from the fawn and took a step backward.

"Let's leave it," Henry said. "The mother is close by. She'll come take care of her own baby if we give her room."

"Are you sure?"

He smiled. "Mothers don't go far. But they're a lot more worried about people than that fawn is, and she won't come back until we're out of the way." Pointing toward the roadway, he said, "I'll walk with you. Let's give the deer some room, though."

As we moved through the fern bed and back to the scraggly brush nearer the road, I asked Henry, "When did you see me?"

"Today," he said mildly.

"But where? Where was I when you saw me?"

He tilted his head sideways, looking at me a moment, and stopped walking. "When you first stood behind the poplar," he said at last. "I was up the slope some, but I caught a bit of the color of your skirt and wandered over."

"Did anyone else see me?" The question was urgent; if my father had seen me, or even any of the boys from the village, I might be in trouble.

Henry paused and thought. "I don't believe anyone else did," he decided. "You might say they were busy looking the other way."

"Good." I sighed, and started walking again. "Anyway, I'm glad to see you. I wanted to ask you something."

"About baskets?" he guessed.

"No. Umm, you see, my mother has this cough. Sort of all the time. And I know my grandmother takes care of her, and I know she's drinking tea and all, but it's not getting better, it's getting worse. So I just wondered"—I scuffed a foot, embarrassed— "well, I wondered, and please don't tell my grandmother I said this, but I wondered if there were some other kinds of tea that maybe my grandmother didn't know. And you might," I finished quickly. He probably thought I was crazy. My face burned, and I stopped at the edge of the muddy road.

Henry stopped, too. "I don't think so," he said slowly. "Everyone knows how your grandmother grows things and gathers things. I don't think I would know anything your grandmother doesn't know. And I'm not as old, of course, so I'm not as wise. Still," he drew the word out, thinking, "I wonder whether your mother might want to go to Lunenburg, to the sweat lodge maybe. Sometimes that draws dangerous things back out. Eh?"

The little French Canadian twist of "Eh" on the end made me smile. I shook my head. "I don't think my mother ever goes to a sweat lodge. So there is one where your family goes in the summer?" I'd heard of them, but in books, not at home. Indians used to use them in the old days. I thought it was for braves, though, Indians who were going to war. I said so to Henry.

He pursed his lips. "Maybe out West it could be for warriors, but not here. At least, that's not how it is for the Abenaki, or not in these days. But the sweat lodge will break a fever, and I know some people who go into the lodge even more than that, to get clear inside, somehow. Why don't you ask your grandmother if it might help?"

"I will. Thanks."

He began to speak again, then hesitated.

"What is it?"

"Well, it's just that I keep wondering," he said slowly. "Wondering why, when your grandmother knows the old ways so well, the rest of your family doesn't know as much. Your father?"

I didn't like the question. "My father's busy," I said with some irritation. "He works hard in the woods. He doesn't have time for plants and ceremonies or whatever. He's a good person!"

Henry closed his eyes a moment, then opened them and said, "I knew that question would come out wrong. Everyone else says he's a good man, too, Molly, that's not what I mean. I guess I mean, how do you choose who to be when you're not really Abenaki?"

"How do you mean, I'm not really Abenaki?" My voice rose. It hadn't mattered to me before, because I'd rather not have been called Frenchy or had my skin be so dark in summer, but how could Henry question who I was? "My father's family is a hundred percent Abenaki, and my mother's family is halfway," as my mother's family had been "mixed" French Canadian, up in Quebec. I continued, "So I'm Abenaki, too. I am!"

"No, you're not."

I wanted to slap at Henry for saying that. *What a stupid thing to say!* I grabbed hold around myself with my arms and took one deep breath, and fought my voice down enough to ask without shouting, "What do you think I am, then?"

"Born to be Abenaki," he now agreed. "But not raised in it." I couldn't say he was wrong about that part, not really. He read my face and went on: "Imagine snow, and what it takes to make it into a snowman. Or milk becoming ice cream. You have to add something to it. You have to learn it," he insisted.

Stuck-up. Arrogant. Ignorant. Mean. The words piled up on my tongue and in my chest. For a sharp, clear moment, I hated Henry for saying I wasn't Indian, as much as I'd ever hated anyone who said I was! Besides, it was all my mother's fault that I didn't know more of the old ways, wasn't it? A burst of anger tightened my chest and I whirled around, ready to leave.

Abruptly, Henry sat down on a log and stared at his feet. "Now I don't know how to undo what I've said," he mourned. "I know I shouldn't have said it like that." He looked up at me. "I don't know how. Teach me. Please."

I looked back at him. Nothing could have surprised me more. Henry the calm, Henry who knew so much, even about me, was asking me for help. And I was just angry enough to not want to help him.

Then again—at least he admitted he'd done something wrong. I sighed, and sat down after all. "You don't have a right to tell anyone what they are or are not," I spelled out. "You can ask questions, but you can't use them to make labels on people. Not on me, anyway. And," I concluded firmly, "if you want to stay friends with me, you have to pay attention to what I just said, and you have to say you're sorry."

A long empty moment hung after my words. I thought, *He can't do it. He can't apologize.* I wanted to cry, not because of being hurt but because if he couldn't do that one thing, what kind of friend could he be for me?

But at last he lifted his face and looked right into mine. "I'm sorry," he said quietly. "Keep teaching me about friendship. I want to be your friend. Always."

In the tremble in his voice, I heard something more. It comforted me in a deep place. I suddenly knew that going to the dance with Eddie, even along with Katy and Jimmy, wasn't right for me. But I'd already said I would go. I sighed, too, unwilling to explain. Instead I just confirmed, looking into Henry's dark eyes, "Good. We're friends, then. I'm glad."

"And I am too."

The unspoken possibilities made my mouth dry. I could feel the next step in front of me: a touch of hands, or even a kiss. But it was too soon, at least for me, so very carefully, without brushing against his hand or shirt, I stood up and gestured toward the path. Henry stood up, too, a half smile lingering on his face. We turned together toward the truck road, where there was barely room for one person to walk the center ridge, out of the mud holes. I walked first, and Henry followed. I listened to the soft swish of his clothes and gentle pad of his feet in the damp grass.

Over one shoulder I asked my own question: "I thought you were going out to Lancaster or Lunenburg for the summer. For baskets and all."

Whatever that "all" was for his family who was some- how much more Abenaki than my family. I'd heard about the summer camp, where people who held the old ways gathered. I added, "But you're still here."

"Mmm. My mother's gone there. And my sister and brothers. I might stay here awhile and work on the farm."

"With your father?"

"Mmm. Yes. The cooking's not as good, but we get a lot done."

"Oh."

We reached the main road, and it was a relief, as all the time I'd been worried that some truck from the dam site might come up behind us. Walking together was comfortable now, easy.

"You're not working at the dam, though? Why not? All the other boys—and men—seem to be down there this summer."

A long moment of silence rode again between us. Finally Henry replied, "I don't mind the lake com- ing. I like a lake. But I'm not sure the spirits of the river do. I guess I won't help put the dam there, just in case."

To me that made a strange sort of sense. It also made me think of Gratia. What was it that linked her and the river? Was it just the way she died? What would happen when the river became swollen with a lake in the middle of it?

I brushed the thought away. I wanted space without Gratia now. At least, a big part of me did. The part that really did like walking with Henry Laporte, even though it felt so new.

We reached the turn to his farm, and Henry lifted a hand to say good-bye. I lifted mine, too, and for a moment we brushed our palms together, a quick touch that didn't flame but warmed me anyway.

"Bye," I said.

"See you," he promised with a smile, then turned and walked away.

Suddenly remembering Katy, I looked at the sky and guessed it was after three already. I walked faster, part of me already back in the village — and part of me still quiet, crouching in a bed of ferns next to a shivering fawn.

· ✡ ·

Katy sat on the bench by the store entrance, waiting. I hurried up the wooden steps, calling out, "I'm
sorry." But it was only quarter to four, and she was
early, and I wasn't late. She handed me a molasses
cookie, took a bite of her own, and we sat together
in the sunshine. I could feel the sun's rays melting the
last of the anger in my chest, and I drew a long slow
breath. In the back of my mind I noticed the effect,
and thought again of Henry's suggestion about the
steamy sweat lodge for my mother's cough.

To Katy, though, I said, "Strawberries?"

She laughed, that great Irish laugh of hers, and
said, "I know what you mean when you say that, but

do you think anyone else would know? You put a lot of question into one word!"

I laughed with her. "Well?"

"Well, yes, I'm still going to pick them, out at the Williams farm. Mr. Williams came into the store today and said picking is starting Monday. He's already got boys weeding, but he wants a picking crew that's more mature, he said." She pulled back and twinkled at me: "Do you think I'm more mature?"

Grinning, I answered, "It depends whether it's Mr. Williams looking or one of the boys!"

As we both dissolved in giggles, I realized that having Katy leave for teacher's training school in Montpelier was going to be awful. Luckily, a pair of small boys ran up the steps past us, staring, and I fell back into giggling, saying to Katy, "And look how mature *they* think we are!"

When Katy caught her breath again, she said, "I'll be paid twice, you know. Once for picking, and a little bit more from my father for the ones I bring back to the store. What about you? Do you want to pick too?"

I grimaced. "I probably can't. It's going to be wash and iron and fold, all summer long, for me. My mother's already not keeping up as well, and I guess it will be even harder for her as her time gets closer."

Katy nodded solemnly. "It must be hard to be expecting at her age."

"I guess." I hesitated. After all, I didn't really know enough. Maybe that was why Mama's cough kept getting worse. But I didn't really want to talk about my mother. Instead, I said, "I saw Eddie at noon, down by the bridge."

"Fishing, I bet! I heard someone say he works at the dam only about half-time, because he spends all his lunch hours fishing and he leaves work early and gets back late."

"Yeah. Anyway, I told him I'd come to the dance. But not like a date! And that's okay with him too."

"Great!" She nodded at what I hadn't said, and asked, "You went walking with Henry Laporte, didn't you?"

"Twice now," I admitted. "I like him."

Katie peered intently at me. "So, are you seeing him?"

I hesitated. "No, I don't think it's like that. At least—I don't know. I just know I like him. He's nice to walk with. And I don't want Eddie to get any kind of ideas, you know?"

My best friend understood me. "You won't be alone with him. We'll stick together. What are you going to wear?"

Now that was indeed a question. Nothing I owned seemed like what a person would wear to a Saturday night dance. I said so.

"Of course you have things for a dance! You have that white blouse with the soft dropped collar, or the ivory one, and that long blue skirt. And if we both wear long scarves around our necks, we'll look stylish, too."

Hmm. Like the cover of the mystery book I'd taken home earlier. I said, "Can you come over for a while and help me look through my outfits? You always pick them out better than I do. And I've got three different scarves."

"Sure."

So we headed up the main street, then down the river road. A haze of new green leaves softened the trees along the roadside, and small yellow tufts of coltsfoot flowers blossomed at the edge of the grass. From a distance, our house looked perfect, complete with the thick rosebushes at the front. I said, "Did I tell you we're moving?"

"No! Where? And how long have you known

and not told me?" She shook my shoulder in exasperation. "I swear, Molly, you're not a good friend if you keep secrets from me!"

"Just to the house past the library, and not until the end of the summer, and I've hardly even had time to think about it," I answered. "The new lake, it's going to come up past where our house is now. So we have to."

She understood right away. "That's awful! Your room, and your beautiful gardens, and the reading place out back, that's awful!" We stood arm in arm, looking down at the wonderful home that just sat too close to the river.

Katy tugged at my hand. "Wait! Couldn't you just have the house moved? People do that all the time, I've seen it!"

Hope flared for a moment, then ashed. "Probably not in the village," I admitted. "People move houses across farms mostly. And I can't see how anything could pull it up this hill, anyway."

More slowly, subdued, we walked down the hill. I thought about telling Katy how things with Henry were going. Something stopped me, though: Katy's differentness was her Irishness, and being Catholic. She'd grown up with the Catholic part, just about a hundred percent, but now her family sometimes went to church in Waterford. She would be less different each year. Me, if I kept walking with Henry and thinking about what it meant to be Abenaki, well, I might be headed toward being *more* different instead. How could I explain all that to my best friend?

There wasn't time even to start. As we came close to the porch, I heard my mother coughing, coughing, coughing. I threw a glance of apology at Katy and pushed ahead of her into the kitchen. "Mama?"

My mother was leaning over the dry sink, coughing so hard I thought she'd choke. "Mama!" I dashed some water into a cup and held it toward her. "Mama, drink something; you can't keep coughing like that." I looked around for my grandmother and called out "Me-Mere?" but she didn't answer. My mother sipped a bit of water, pointed toward the river, then began again to cough. I looked at the cloth she was holding to her face and realized there were flecks of blood in the fabric. Frightened, I urged her toward a chair.

And just as she went to sit on it, with Katy at one side of her, me at the other, she suddenly cried out, a long, frightened wail.

"Mama! What is it?"

Coughing again, collapsing onto the chair, she gestured desperately at her skirt, tears running down her cheeks. "Get Me-Mere!" she choked out between coughs. "Hurry!"

I stared at the blood seeping through the skirt fabric, unable for a long moment to grasp what was happening.

"The baby," Katy hissed. "She's losing the baby. Run, find your grandmother. I'll wait here with her."

I ran.

I ran out the door and down the hill toward the river, for that was the direction my mother had pointed while she stood at the sink. But I didn't see Me-Mere. Looking upriver, looking downriver, no. Where was she?

Someone tapped my shoulder and I jumped and spun — and it was Henry. "You were running," he said urgently, out of breath himself. "I saw you from the store. What's wrong?"

"My mother," I gasped. "She's losing the baby. I have to find my grandmother."

"I know where she is," he called out, already running north along the riverbank, toward the covered bridge. "Go home, take care of your mother, I'll get your grandmother!"

I raced back up the hill, and there in front of my house, just turning into the yard, were the two nurses that had visited the school. I pushed past them, still running. "My mother's sick," I tossed toward them. And in a flurry of starched white skirts, they followed me into the house.

"Williams, get another chair and put her feet up on it," snapped the older nurse, quickly taking charge. Katy moved to the side, holding a blood-flecked towel and an empty water glass. Toward me, the older nurse demanded, "Clean towels and a clean sheet. Now!"

I dodged around two baskets of fresh-ironed wash and raced up the stairs to our chest of linens in the hall and took all the towels out of it, four of them, and an ironed white sheet. After nearly falling as I rushed downstairs with them, I swung around the railing and sped back to the kitchen.

As I handed the linens to the younger nurse, the older one knelt next to my mother and lifted her bloodied skirt and petticoat, folding them out of the way. She asked my mother something, and I heard Mama say "nearly seven months" between coughs that shook her and forced out more water and blood from between her legs.

"Oh, dear," said the older nurse, "I'm sorry," and she pulled my mother's underpants down rapidly and began to pack the folded towels against her private parts, pressing. My mother cried out.

"Don't hurt her!" I yelled, tugging at the nurse's arm. She brushed me aside.

"I'm trying to save the baby," she snapped. "Get out of the way. Williams, move the girl aside. And get some water—we've got to stop the coughing." She glared at Katy. "Is the blood on that cloth from below, or from the cough?"

"The, the cough," Katy stammered.

"Aha! Williams, water—what's taking so long?"

I was almost afraid for the younger nurse, the older one sounded so angry. Thinking quickly, I jumped up and got the jar of honey out of the cupboard and dipped a spoon into it. I brought the honey-filled teaspoon over to my mother, who was trying to sip the water but coughing too hard, so it ran out of her mouth, much the way the water and blood were surging out of the other end of her.

"Mama," I said urgently, "I've got some honey." The younger nurse, Williams, moved out of the way and patted my shoulder as I knelt to touch the spoon to my mother's mouth. Her tongue flicked out, and it did, it did work, the honey did work for a moment.

"Good," snapped the older nurse. "Do it again. And breathe, Mrs.—girl, what is your mother's name?"

She was asking Katy, who pointed at me. Katy said, "It's Molly's mother, not mine. Mrs. Ballou."

"Mrs. Ballou, can you hear me? Don't try to speak, just nod your head. I don't want you coughing again. Hold some of that honey in your mouth, try to calm down." She held my mother's gaze intently, never letting go of the folded towel that she was pushing between my mother's legs. She added, "I'm Nurse Carpenter, that's Nurse Williams. We'll try to save the baby, but I'm not sure we can. So you have to try hard, too."

I turned to Katy. "Henry Laporte's getting my grandmother. Can you try to find my father?" I glanced at the clock. "He might even be at the store. The work shift might be over." It was quarter past five.

Katy nodded and headed for the door, where someone was knocking. Mrs. Wheeler stood just outside. "What's wrong?" she asked, moving into the kitchen. "What can I do to help?"

I suddenly realized she'd come for her wash. I gestured toward the baskets. "Can you take those out, Mrs. Wheeler? And please, could you help Katy find my father?"

"Of course." In a whirl of skirts she was back out the door, basket of ironed sheets in hand and

Katy carrying the second basket. I heard the bang of a truck door and the grind of its starter, and turned back to my mother, dipping another spoonful of honey and trying to help her with it. She licked at the spoon, then coughed again.

"Water," my mother whispered, and Nurse Williams bent close with the glass, tipping it gently so Mama could swallow some. Then I put the honey spoon back against her lip.

"Williams!" came an order from the other nurse. "Spread the clean sheet on the kitchen table. The baby's head is crowning."

Crowning? What did she mean? I stared, while the younger nurse, without questions, moved quickly to cover our kitchen table with the sheet I'd brought. Suddenly I was helping the two nurses to lift my mother up onto the table. She wasn't as heavy as she looked, and with such panic in my arms, it wasn't hard to help lift her. I heard the clink of the honeyed spoon dropping to the floor behind me. We barely had my mother moved up onto the table before her cough started again.

"Pillow!" the older nurse demanded, and this time I raced into Me-Mere's bedroom beyond the kitchen, to get the closest one, and tucked it beneath my mother's head. The sweat running down her face frightened me.

"Mama?"

"Don't try to talk with her," Nurse Carpenter ordered. "She'll cough more. You shouldn't even be here, girl—what's your name, Molly? But if you want to stay, get more honey on a clean spoon. Stay by your mother's head, try to help her not to cough."

I did what I was told. Shaking, I held Mama's face toward me and eased the honey into her lips, over and over, sometimes holding the water there instead, in another spoon. Looking only into Mama's weeping, red face, I tried to hold her eyes with mine, and stroked her hair, and whispered, "You can do it, Mama. Don't cough again. You can hold it back."

Behind me, at Mama's other end, I heard the nurses working and talking with each other in low voices, but I tried not to look. If I looked, I knew I'd be even more scared, and Mama would see it in my face. I forced all my love for my mother into my face instead and kept stroking her hair and trying to help her to sip the water, lick the honey, hold still.

A sudden cramp seized her, all of her, her head rising from the pillow. She cried out, then screamed.

"Mama!" I screamed in response. "Mama, Mama!"

"If you can't be quiet, you need to leave, right now," the older nurse yelled at me. "Be quiet, Molly, or get out of this kitchen right now!"

I gasped the sound back into my throat and leaned forward, holding my mother's shoulders, trying to comfort her as the rest of her body struggled and seized and fought. I knew what must be happening: the baby, the little baby, was being born.

"Too soon, too soon," went the chant in my mind. And "Mama, Mama," I whispered aloud. "Don't cough, Mama. Don't cry."

I smelled the hot blood smell, and another smell, as Mama soiled herself. I turned my head for a quick look and saw the nurses frantically moving to clean her and hold something that was being pushed out of her, between her legs. I stared. Was it the baby?

My mother began to cough again in my arms, then sob, and I could only hold her and say, "Don't cry, don't cry, Mama, please." I tried to find the honeyed spoon, but it was lost. Crying myself, I held her and felt her press the rest of the baby outward into the hands of the nurses.

A hand on my shoulder pulled at me, and I blinked my eyes to see my grandmother, at last. "Me-Mere!"

"I'm here," she confirmed. "I'll hold her now. Let go."

My mother looked into my grandmother's grim, pinched face. "Too soon," she whispered, and coughed again.

"Too soon," my grandmother agreed sadly. "Come here, come," she whispered as she wrapped my mother's face in her soft arms.

I stepped back, sobbing, rubbing at my own face with half-numb hands, the feeling gone out of them from holding Mama so tightly. An arm reached gently across my shoulder and turned me. Against the scratchy cloth of Henry Laporte's shirt, I wept, and gave up trying to be strong.

"My father?" I finally asked, sniffing, pulling back and fumbling for a handkerchief. He gave me one from his pocket.

"Mrs. Wheeler and Katy are driving to the dam to get him," Henry answered quietly. He pulled me toward the other side of the kitchen and pressed a glass of water into my hand. "Drink it," he urged.

I took a swallow, and blew my nose again, and wiped at my face, where my eyes kept streaming as if the tears had no end.

Now I looked at the nurses at last. One, the older one, still worked between my mother's legs. The other, Nurse Williams, I remembered, was wrapping a tiny baby in a towel.

She looked up at me and brought the small bundle across the room. "It was a little brother," she whispered. "You may kiss him if you like. I'm afraid he's not breathing." Suddenly she noticed Henry and directed him to sit over in the corner, out of the way.

I looked at the tiny, doll-size face. Feathers of dark hair cupped the little head, under the towel. I held out a tentative hand to touch the miniature pale-gray cheek.

I looked up into the nurse's face. She looked sad, almost as sad as I felt. She said quietly, "Would you like to hold him?" I nodded, and she put the bundle into my arms, which I cuddled as if there were a breathing, fragile baby in the wrapped towel.

And it was, in fact, a baby. My mother's baby. My little brother. He was warm inside the towel, and it was hard to believe there was no life in his little form. I bent my face toward him and smelled the mix of scents, skin smell and blood and something else I couldn't place, something as heavy and dark as the insides of a heart. And laundry smell, soap and fresh air, from the towel. Gently, I kissed the tiny forehead.

My grandmother pressed up to my shoulder, peering into the baby's face also. She said quietly, "Let me hold him now." And I passed the baby to her.

Then I looked at my mother, still on the kitchen table. And suddenly she was all that mattered—not the baby, not the other people in the room. Her face, so damp and red before, now looked pale and thin and empty, and I hurried across to hold her.

"We need to get her into bed," the older nurse said quietly. "She needs to be kept warm."

The younger nurse said something to the older one that I didn't quite hear, as my mother began to cough again.

"Yes," said the older nurse. "Yes, tuberculosis, clearly. Which is why she miscarried."

Again Nurse Williams whispered something, and Nurse Carpenter nodded. "While they make the bed ready," she answered. And she turned to me and Henry and my grandmother and said, "Is there a bedroom on this floor of the house?"

My grandmother nodded. "Use mine," she told me. I looked at Henry, and he walked with me to the other room, where together we folded down the blankets on my grandmother's narrow bed. I looked around the room, thinking about whether there were things I should hide before the nurses came in. I swept clothes onto a chair and tucked underneath them a pair of birch-bark baskets. Henry picked up the feathers from the top of the dresser and gently laid them into the top drawer. We nodded at each other and started back to the kitchen.

A cry of pain from my mother made me run. My grandmother, still holding the wrapped dead baby, called out, "What are you doing to her?" And Nurse Williams stood between us and Nurse Carpenter, whose hands were between my mother's legs.

"Cleaning," said Nurse Williams quickly. "Cleaning out the afterbirth. So there won't be an infection."

My grandmother accepted the explanation and moved back to the other side of the kitchen, rocking the baby and crooning something to it. But I stepped closer to my mother instead and saw a sharp flash of a blade in Nurse Carpenter's hand.

"Stop it!" I called out. "You're hurting her!"

She turned her face toward me, eyes blazing. "It has to be done" was all she said, as she tugged a handful of bleeding flesh out of my mother's most private place, and blood, too much blood, flew forth in a dark red wave onto the sheet-covered table.

Swiftly wrapping the handful of bloody something into a towel, along with the blade, the nurse snapped to me, "Another towel, if you want to help her."

I ran and passed the last towel to her, and as she

stuffed it between my mother's legs, she reached with her other wet bloodied hand and seized mine, placing it on my mother's stomach. "Press here," she ordered. "You need to press here, to help stop the bleeding."

With all my heart and strength, I pressed.

My father came running in the door just after we all had carried Mama to Me-Mere's bed. I heard him and went back to the kitchen, with Henry behind me. Papa stood there in the doorway a long moment, stunned. I turned to look around, seeing what he must be seeing: the blood-covered table; the gouts of blood on the floor; my grandmother rocking in the corner with the baby bundle, her eyes shut and an Abenaki chant coming from her in a whisper. So what he said first made sense to me: "Your mother. Is she—is she alive?"

"Yes," I choked out. "Yes, Papa. But the baby's dead, and Mama's bleeding, and I'm so scared. Papa, do something!" I gestured toward the back bedroom, and he regained movement, hurrying across the kitchen. Henry followed him, saying something quiet.

Me-Mere hadn't even looked up.

Discouraged, exhausted, still terrified, I did the only thing I could think to do: I poured hot water from the ever-heating kettle at the back of the stove into a bowl, added soap, and picked up one of the bloodied towels, meaning to wash it out and begin to mop up the floor.

Mrs. Wheeler and Katy, who'd been standing outside the doorway, came inside then and began to help me clean. Katy asked me first, "Are you bleeding, too, Molly? Are you hurt?"

I looked down at my clothes, bloodstained from helping to move Mama to the bedroom. "No," I said wearily. "Only in my heart."

Mrs. Wheeler caught back a sob and pulled me against her narrow chest for a moment, then stepped across the room to look into the baby's face as my grandmother continued to rock and sing. She didn't try to touch him, or my grandmother, though. And then she turned to the kitchen table, folding up the sheet and towels there, while Katy and I wiped every surface around us, and we all sniffled as we labored. And though Mrs. Wheeler wore a nice blue dress, I saw that she only rolled up the sleeves, working as hard in her good clothing as the two of us in our summer run-about skirts and blouses, and I thought, *She is a kind person. And she isn't even family.*

Nor was Henry, but somehow it felt right to have him there, maybe because I knew he saw things the way my grandmother did: full of moons and plants and seasons. And birds.

Henry and my father came out of the back bedroom together, talking in low voices. I heard my father say, "The minister will want to come," and Henry nodded. My father concluded, "So, not until Friday, I think." They nodded to each other.

"I'll ask them to telephone, then, from the store," Henry said. He turned to me and added, "I'm sorry, Molly, I need to go down to the store while there's still someone there, to call your uncles. I'll be back in the morning, though."

I lifted a hand to say good-bye. This time he didn't touch my hand, but he lifted his own and I could almost feel that same warmth. "In the morning, then," I answered him, and he left the house.

Without speaking, my grandmother stood and put the wrapped baby into my father's arms, and it was his turn to sit and rock, tears running down his cheeks. Me-Mere rubbed her face a moment, then walked back to her bedroom. A few minutes later, the two nurses finally came out to the kitchen.

The younger one, Nurse Williams, looked tired and sad; the older one looked around the room as if it were a bad place. Maybe it was the spatters of blood and boot mud still on some parts of the floor, and the sour smell of the mound of soiled towels and sheets. Maybe it was more. I was too tired to be sure.

Since nobody else spoke up, I took a deep breath and said, "Thank you. Thank you for helping my mother. I know you tried to save my—my brother." It was hard to say it out loud. "Thank you for trying."

Nurse Carpenter cleared her throat loudly. "Your mother," she pronounced firmly, "has tuberculosis, and I believe your grandmother has it too. Consumption," she added, to be clear. "And at her age, I assure you, she should not have tried to carry a baby." My father tipped his face a moment to look up, then steadied his rocking and kept on, saying nothing.

What should I say to this nurse, this woman who told me my parents did something wrong? Did she blame us for the baby dying? Was she angry?

She continued, "Keep your mother warm, and make sure to change the towels for clean ones every hour. Nurse Williams and I will visit her tomorrow to check for fever. Your mother needs to drink fluids, clear ones like tea and broth, no milk, and she needs to stay in bed for at least two weeks. After that, she should go to the hospital in St. Johnsbury to see the doctors about the tuberculosis. Your whole family should go."

"Yes, ma'am," I replied. I didn't mean we'd go, just that I heard her, and I wanted her to go away. "Thank you, ma'am."

Mrs. Wheeler was wringing out towels at the sink but I saw she was listening. I said, "Mrs. Wheeler? I appreciate what you've done for us, ma'am, and we all thank you. And I was wondering, would you be able to take the nurses to"—I paused, unsure— "Where do you need to go?" I asked them.

Nurse Carpenter answered, "We are boarding with Mrs. Wells. At this hour, a ride would certainly be appreciated."

Mrs. Wheeler nodded her white-haired head, dried her hands, and said she also would come back in the morning. "Try to get some rest tonight, dear," she told me kindly. "Tomorrow will be a long and challenging day."

As she and the nurses left, I saw the sun was low. It must be late, then, close to seven o'clock already. I didn't know where the evening had gone, or what

215

to do about supper, or anything. I sagged into a chair and looked around at the cleaning still to be done, at my father curled in the rocking chair with our baby, and at the empty top of the stove, where supper should have been cooking.

A knock at the door startled me. It was Katy; I hadn't even realized she was gone. In her hands she held a covered dish.

"My mother sent a casserole," she explained. "And I can stay the night if you want me to."

Yes. Yes, I did want her to.

Together we set the kitchen table and filled a tray for my grandmother, who stayed in the bedroom, nursing Mama. And when we had the dishes all washed, the floor scrubbed, and the last bundle of towels soaking in a soapy bucket of water, we climbed the stairs together, moved the blankets and pillows from my bed onto the floor so we could share them, and slept in our damp shifts.

The sound of horses in the road and knocking at our barely used front door woke me early the next morning, Wednesday. What a lot of things had changed since the morning before. I heard the front door open, and my father's voice and another man's. Wearily, I stood and dug out a fresh blouse to wear, tiptoeing so that Katy could rest a little longer. By the light outside, it was barely seven, a bright mid-summer morning so different from what I felt that it didn't make any sense at all.

Down the stairs I went, into the first full day of grieving. The minister sat with my father at the kitchen table, and half a dozen dishes of food had already arrived, lined up along the other side of the table. Coffee steamed at the back of the stove.

A small wooden box sat on the floor by the porch door. My baby brother's coffin, I realized. Although I thought I had cried enough the day before, I felt my eyes swell and drip, and I ran back up to my room to get my handkerchief. I brought down all that I had, placing them in a stack in the hall, where I could reach them easily.

Then I waited for a gap in the minister's conversation with my father, to ask, "Mama?"

My father nodded. "With your grandmother. But let them rest for now."

Three days.

The Reverend Witherspoon wanted to bury the baby on Thursday morning, but my father persuaded him to wait for Friday, three days from my little brother's arrival in the light of the sun. Relatives arrived steadily all day Wednesday and part of Thursday. My grandmother guarded the back bedroom fiercely, so that even my aunts and I could visit only for a moment at a time, to stroke my mother's pale hand or kiss her cheek, alternately flushed with fever and white with loss. When Me-Mere came to the kitchen one time for more tea, I asked her, "Is the fever from the baby or from what the nurses said—tuberculosis? Consumption?"

Me-Mere puffed angrily but kept her voice low. "Those nurses don't know the difference between consumption and a spring cough. Your mother only has a cough—and childbed fever, and a part of her misses that baby so much that she'll be slow to heal."

She cut off her words and looked hard at me, and I whispered, "Gratia. Two babies." Me-Mere nodded. We understood each other.

The nurses, who indeed returned on Wednesday morning, were firmly turned away at the door by my father. Neighbors brought food and retreated, letting us know they cared but staying out of the way.

Katy stayed on with me through these days, until late on Friday afternoon, when the small grave at the village cemetery had closed and the cousins and uncles and aunts, murmuring final scraps of Abenaki wishes for healing, climbed back into their automobiles and trucks and wagons and left, for St. Albans and Guildhall and Canada. And the last thing Katy said before she went home on Friday night was, "I'll come over in the morning. We have to talk about the dance."

The dance? Oh. Saturday, and the dance.

I shook my head. "I'm too tired to think about it," I admitted. "We can talk tomorrow. But probably I won't be able to go." She hugged me without

219

pushing the idea any further and slipped quietly out the door.

Then for me the real darkness of Friday night began, the first night that my family sat alone with the sorrow that choked our house and our throats.

It seemed impossible that there was still light in the world. Almost nine o'clock, and the sky glowed with the last of the summer day. Inside our house, shadows grew thicker. Me-Mere came into the kitchen for a bowl of cool water to wash my mother's face and hands. My father stood, weaving a bit on his feet, black suit hanging loose from his shoulders.

I moved up against him with a hug, and gently he rubbed the top part of my back before patting my head. Poor Papa! There was no way for him to make the world right or safe after all. And neither of us had any strength left to comfort the other. But he was still my father, and I wanted him to show me how to go forward.

"Get some sleep, Molly," was what he told me now. "Tomorrow's another day. There's nothing we can do tonight."

"I want to wipe down the table first," I replied.

He nodded, and after a slow questioning look toward my grandmother's bedroom, where my mother lay, he shook his head a bit and started up the stairs. I moved to wring a cloth out in hot water and began to scrub the table, the chairs, and to wipe the boards by the sink, then set the table for breakfast. Better than sitting still, better than worrying about Mama. Only Me-Mere knew what to do for Mama.

Somehow I couldn't shut the door to the porch; the darkening kitchen grew small and tight around me, and I needed to breathe. I stepped outside.

Honeysuckle scent hung in the twilight, and robins persisted in calling from the trees, despite the hour. I could hear the river, too, splashing past. The strawberry moon, half-swollen toward fullness, peeked above the hills to the east, against a pale blue-gray sky.

A lamp at my parents' bedroom window upstairs went out. I walked slowly out of the garden and up the road, away from the river, toward the church, and out to the east to the cemetery where we'd all huddled, surrounded by cousins and aunts and uncles and neighbors, a few hours earlier.

The cemetery gate stood open. I stepped through it, dodging a thorny twig of a rosebush. The scented air here hung more damply, especially near the mound of soil over the small, new grave. The plain stone just past it said "Gratia."

Would this baby have a stone with a name?

I sat on the damp ground. The dew soaked into my skirt. Eyes dry, out of tears, I leaned my face into my hands. No little sister voice rose up, no challenge or blame from the older sister who'd never grown up. I wondered if her spirit was somewhere with the baby. Picturing her, holding the tiny hand, comforted me a little.

Behind me, over by the gate, someone said quietly, "Can I help?"

I wasn't surprised to realize it was Henry. I stood and turned, brushing off my skirt awkwardly.

"Are you still watching me?" I asked him, curious and touched.

"Not exactly," he said slowly. "It just seems like, where I walk, a lot of the time I find you."

After a moment I replied, "That's nice, Henry. But I was sitting alone, and maybe I need that sometimes."

He nodded. "But maybe not now, Molly. Maybe now is still a time to be with someone. Besides"— he looked around —"I'm not sure this is a place where anyone is alone."

That felt strange, but good, too: thinking of the people in the cemetery keeping each other company. I remembered what my aunts had called the burying place: the forest of coffins.

"My chest aches," I explained. "I didn't know I'd miss that baby so much, when I hadn't even met him yet."

"Mmm."

Past Henry's head, I saw the moon had risen over the trees and was lighting the village. Everything looked pale, and tender, and oddly safe. I could not hear the river as a separate sound, just a distant chorus of spring frogs questioning the night.

Henry walked me home, and I turned into the walk to the kitchen door on my own. Standing on the porch, I watched him give a small wave and head back up the hill, toward his own family. I wondered what he told them about us. About me. They must have asked him, this week at least.

I was too tired to think about it more. It took all my strength to go up the stairs, pull off my clothes, and wash just enough before slipping into bed.

I was grateful not to wake with any dreams.

·�֎·

On Saturday morning, my best friend, my father, and my grandmother all joined in telling me what to do. And they all said: "Go to the dance."

Actually Katy only asked; it was my grandmother who pushed. She even said she'd iron my best blouse and skirt while my father took a turn sitting with my mother in the back bedroom. My father nodded, asking only whether the boys would pick me up at our house and who was driving.

So at six o'clock on Saturday evening, feeling like a deserter for walking away from my stricken family, I pulled on my best blouse and skirt, fastened my silver locket around my neck and tucked it under the blouse, then knotted a long silky scarf that Katy had loaned to me. Swinging back and forth to catch my reflection in the narrow pier glass, I guessed it would do. With the scarf, I thought I looked a little like one of the women aviators. And the hollows of my cheeks from this terrible week only made me look more adult somehow. I pinched at my face to make my cheeks red. Pride made me want to look good. No one at the dance, besides Katy, would know my heart was numb.

I went to say good-bye to my mother; my grandmother sat next to her, with a pile of mending, a faint fragrance of cedar and sage in the room telling me there'd been some native medicine at work. I lifted an eyebrow at Me-Mere and sniffed loudly; she only shrugged. "There's a time to comb out your hair and look pretty, and a time to work harder than that," she said cryptically.

Kissing my mother lightly on the forehead didn't wake her. I grieved that she was too sick to see me dressed for my first dance. Her skin felt hot, and I asked Me-Mere in a whisper, "Fever?" She nodded, then unexpectedly stood up and beckoned to me to come out of the room.

Outside the door, she bent close to me and whispered, "Those nurses cut her up inside."

"No, Me-Mere, they just took the afterbirth out," I whispered back. "I asked someone. You have to take it out or you can die afterward."

"More," my grandmother pronounced firmly. "They did more. They cut her up. There'll be no more babies." Anger and sorrow flamed in her eyes.

"She's too old for more babies, isn't she?"

"She wasn't too old for this one, was she? No, they cut her up on purpose. They don't want Indian babies around here."

In shock, my voice rose, and Me-Mere lifted a quick hand to my lips, hushing me. I hissed, "That can't be so. They're nurses. They're supposed to help people!"

"Didn't help her. Think about it. What were they doing in town to start with?"

And spinning on her heels, she slipped back into the bedroom, ignoring me.

I thought about it. Could it be true? New England for Yankees, Vermont for real Vermonters? My mother's dark skin and the slender braid twisted into her hair said Abenaki, surely. But nurses? Would nurses really do such a terrible thing?

Suspicion led to fear, and fear to wanting to stay home, take care of my family, be safe. And then anger took over. I would go to the dance anyway. I was enough of a Vermonter to do what everyone else did. But heaven help those nurses if I ever saw them again, I promised myself.

Unsettled, I stood by the porch door. My father called out, "Did you forget something?" He stepped into view, nodded as he looked at me, and cleared his throat. A half smile forced its way onto his face: "You look nice. Try to have a good time tonight, Molly. We'll be all right here." He looked up the road and said, "Where are your friends?"

Quietly I replied, "I'm early, Papa. I'll walk up to the main road, so the noise won't bother Mama. See you later." He kept the half smile in place and gave a short nod, and I knew he was trying, in his own way, to make things safe and right again. I would do my part, too.

I left the porch and walked up the hill to meet Katy at the store, where Jimmy and Eddie soon arrived to pick us up. Again the top of the Model T Ford was folded down, and the boys sat in front, dressed in pressed shirts and ties with their hair slicked down. They both climbed out to open the doors for us. I didn't know what to say, after being so drowned in sadness for so long, but they both were gentle: Jimmy saying, "Sorry for your loss," and Eddie Beck asking how my mother was doing.

"She's pretty sick," I admitted.

Everyone looked unhappy. Katy squeezed my hand, then rescued me by changing the topic: "Someone tell Molly and me about the dance hall—we've never been there before."

Eddie grinned at Jimmy, who bounced behind the wheel. Jimmy said, "It's the greatest place. All the kids go there now in the summer. The band is from Boston, and the floor sways up and down when the crowd starts swinging."

"Up and down?"

Eddie turned in his seat and beamed at me. "The dance floor hangs right over the lake," he explained eagerly. "It moves like you're on a boat or something. It's the best!"

Katy said she'd heard about it, too. "I can hardly wait!"

"You mean nothing holds up the other end of the floor?" I worried. "What if it breaks and everyone falls in the water?"

"Big beams," Eddie asserted. "Really big ones. Whole trees, really. They're not going to break. But if you're that scared"—he winked at me—"well, we can dance at the safe end, you know. Or I could just hold on to you so you won't fall in!"

I felt my face flame into a blush as I struggled to

think of what to say. I knew I should tease back, but I didn't know how.

Katy spoke up for me. "Who says she's dancing with you the whole time, Eddie Beck? Boy, you're making a big assumption!"

"Whoops!" Jimmy dug a fist into Eddie's shoulder. "You're in trouble now, boy! Better be nice to these girls, or you won't be dancing after all!"

Driving out of the village, west toward Barnet, we passed the turn to the Laporte farm, and I wondered whether Henry ever went to dances or anything. Probably he stayed around home in the evenings, I guessed. But I didn't really know for sure, did I? And after all, I'd seen him in the village in the evening.

But there was too much to see and look forward to now, and I put thoughts of Henry aside for another time. In spite of the summer heat, Katy and I tugged the blanket over our good clothes to keep off the road dust and sat close enough to talk over the roar of the automobile in short bursts. She told me the biggest news of the village, that the dam was being closed off next week, so the lake would begin to grow. When would our house be threatened by the water, I wondered. I'd ask my father later.

The gravel road rose up over the mountain, steep and narrow, past hill farms with the barns still lit up for milking, and the roar of milking machines greeted us at nearly every curve. Going down the far side to East Barnet tipped my half-empty stomach far enough that I gripped the leather hand strap by the door with all my might and closed my eyes for the steepest parts. But Jimmy didn't go too fast, and nobody else seemed to worry.

We drove across the railroad tracks and soon were in the village of Barnet, where shop windows advertised shoes, portrait photography, and groceries. And then it was a smooth five miles along the river to reach West Barnet and Harvey's Lake. As we got close to the lake and the dance pavilion, other cars and trucks slowed us down, until we became part of a long line waiting to park along the sandy strip of beach.

Eddie gave a grand flourishing bow as he opened my door, and I climbed out, tugging my skirt smooth and trying to look in all directions at once. There were so many people there—why, there must have been at least a hundred cars!

Eddie's hand was on my arm, I noticed, as he was still "being a gentleman" by the car door. I turned a little toward the car, so that the space between us widened, and pretended to check my hair in the reflection in the car window; I didn't want to hurt his feelings, but also I'd said I wasn't coming as his date—so his hand on my arm felt wrong. It's just Eddie Beck, I reminded myself, and turned back toward him, trying to smile. We followed behind Katy and Jimmy, who were holding hands, and the four of us wove our way along the shoreline path to the dance pavilion.

Nearly as tall as a village house, it spread widely along the lakeshore, dark boarded sides, small windows wide open, music bouncing out at us. I heard a fiddle and guitars, and thought I heard a piano, too.

All around outside, people stood in small groups, talking and laughing. Some of the men and boys smoked cigarettes, although not the girls. No, I was wrong—there was a girl smoking, and I saw one woman, too, using a long cigarette holder that looked very stylish with her short cap of hair and knee-short skirt. Eddie nudged Jimmy, who was already looking at the woman. I was relieved they didn't say anything though; Katy caught my eye and wrinkled her nose, then grinned, and I smiled back.

The boys paid for us at the doorway, and we stepped into the crowded, thick air, where the music took over my pulse and my breath. Following the others, I squeezed around the dancing group and draped my sweater over a chair to claim it.

"Let's get something to drink," Eddie proposed. I froze a moment, not sure what he meant, then realized there were two big coolers of Coca-Cola at the back end of the room, under a festive set of colored lights. I felt in my pocket for the quarters I'd wrapped in my handkerchief.

"Sure." It was hard to all stay together in the crowd. It was even hard just to keep up with Eddie, and he reached back and took my hand to pull me along. I didn't close my fingers, not wanting to send the wrong message—as soon as there was room, I pulled my hand back and caught up next to him, tucking my hands in my pockets, where they'd be safe.

A song ended, and the crowd dissolved, with couples moving off the dance floor to the chairs and some pushing toward the soft drink coolers, pushing behind us, which brought Eddie and me up to one of them. He reached for a pair of the green glass bottles, pulling them dripping wet out of the pan of ice, and I passed two quarters to the older woman behind the cooler. Eddie was bending to pop the caps off in the opener slot on the cooler, and when he saw me paying, he said, "Hey!"

"My turn," I assured him. "You paid for us to get in." He agreed reluctantly, and we squeezed across to the area against the wall, where there was some space to step through to walk back to our chairs.

The chill fizz and zip of the cola tasted better

232

than ever in the heat and crowd. I heard the band, behind me, starting up again, and laughed to realize I recognized the music, "If You Were the Only Girl in the World."

"Want to dance?" Eddie asked with a lifted eyebrow.

"Not yet," I replied. "Let's drink the Coca-Cola first." It was too romantic a song, anyway. So I watched, and though the noise was powerful and almost deafening, it also saved me from making conversation.

I saw two or three women wearing "flapper" clothes, their short skirts and bare shoulders startling in West Barnet. Most of the girls dressed a lot like Katy and me—some with shorter sleeves on their blouses, and a couple of them with the top button undone to go with the long scarves that swung from their necks.

A man with a saxophone stood next to the piano, and the band pushed into something jazzy, Southern almost. A whoop of delight went up from the crowd, and suddenly people were doing the Charleston. I saw Katy jump up with Jimmy and begin kicking back her heels, slapping her knees through her skirt, and licking her thumbs. Wow, she was good!

Eddie nudged me. "Wanna try?"

"I've never done it," I admitted.

"Me neither." He grinned. "So we can look like beginners together. C'mon, let's go."

He grabbed my hand again and pulled me off my seat. We tried the Charleston holding hands at first, then spun loose and kicked up our feet, laughing at each other. It was hard to hear all the music in the crowded room, but you couldn't miss the beat, as the floor shook with everyone stamping and jumping. I waved to another girl I knew from Waterford, and when she moved closer and danced next to me, I found I was dancing "with her" as well as with Eddie and another boy. Freedom! No push into a romantic couple, just lots of fun.

Two more dances about wore me out, and when the band changed to a slow dance, "Ol' Man River," I sank gratefully onto my chair instead. I passed Eddie my other two quarters, and he went to get more soda pop.

An older man stopped next to my chair and patted my shoulder. "You're a good dancer," he commented. He leaned closer, and I was shocked to smell whiskey on his breath. "You dance almost as good as one of those Negro girls," he purred at me. "Guess your skin's almost dark enough. You're a sweet little Frenchy, aren't you?"

I pulled away, looking for Eddie. "Excuse me, I've got to find my boyfriend," I said rashly, and dashed toward the other end of the room. I ran right into Eddie.

"Here," he said, waving a glass bottle at me, "I didn't know you were in such a hurry for it!"

"Th-thanks," I stammered.

"C'mon, let's go outside and cool off."

Now the sun was down, and the lake glowed with the rose colors of the western sky. Boats drifted around, some with people rowing, some just floating, music coming from one, voices from another. We sat on a big rock by the water, and I felt the night air cooling the sweat off me.

"Umm, Eddie?" I started.

"Yeah?"

"Some man in there—he tried to talk to me and I could smell he'd been drinking. Drinking spirits," I clarified.

Eddie looked embarrassed. "Well, people do, you know. Even with Prohibition, you can buy it if you have the money. And the guys who were drinkers before the law changed are still drinkers now, you see."

"Oh."

"Besides, the law's going to change back anytime now," he added. "It's a bad law. My father says any law you can't enforce is a bad one."

"Hmm."

Some ducks swam over toward us, looking for a handout. We didn't have anything for them. They swam on past. I could hear peepfrogs from the wetland beyond the end of the lake and behind us. Lights sparkled in the windows of summer homes along the water's edge.

Eddie leaned closer. "Are you cold?"

"No, thanks." I stood up quickly. "Let's go dance some more."

He shook his head and patted the rock. "Wait a little longer. I like talking with you, you know?"

I looked uncertainly at him. "Eddie, remember how we said this wouldn't be a date?"

"Sure, sure," he agreed. But he didn't stand up. "Can't we get to know each other, though?"

"I guess."

I sat back down, trying to leave some space between his leg and mine anyway. I pulled my sweater close and buttoned it. "I'm plenty warm," I emphasized. "Dancing warms a person up."

Eddie grinned. "Yeah. I know, I got it, you wanna dance some more. But listen, there's no big rush.

Anyway, I wanted to tell you, I met your father at the dam site. He's nice."

"Thanks. Did he ask you about the dance?"

"Not really, he just said he heard we were all going here. He was telling me about working in the woods last winter, and the river work, you know?"

I was surprised. "Usually he doesn't talk about it, except with my mother. Are you going to the woods next winter?"

He shrugged. "Maybe. There's no river work, but over in New Hampshire they've got train cars for the logs, and I heard there's going to be a spur up to Victory on this side of the river. Your father says the pay is really good."

"I guess." I asked him if he was ever coming back to school, and he said he was done with it. I told him about Miss Webster and surprised myself by telling him about the Montpelier part, too.

"Wow," he said. "Are you going to go there?"

I shook my head. "It's too much money," I explained. "And I'm not really sure I want to be a teacher anyway."

"Yeah, out of the classroom at last, just to be back in school at the other side of the room," he laughed. I laughed, too, and the ducks moved farther out onto the lake, away from our noise.

"You could be my girl, you know," Eddie said quietly. "I'd like that. We could have a real date next time."

I felt bad about saying no again, but I really, really didn't want a date with Eddie, even though he was a nice guy. "I'm sorry," I stumbled, "but Eddie, I just don't want to date anyone yet. Okay?"

"Okay."

So we stood up and went inside the dance hall again. The stiffness from the conversation wore off as we danced more. Some of the tunes I knew, and some were from the new jazz bands, music from Duke Ellington. Eddie knew most of it. One time we danced close enough to Katy and Jimmy to switch, so that I danced part of one with Jimmy, but he was too wild for me. Katy, laughing and flushed, danced like she'd done it all her life. Me, I could feel where a blister had started inside my thick stockings, and I didn't like being all sweaty, and after a while I noticed more people who'd been drinking spirits, maybe somewhere outside. I thought, *I want to go home.*

At last it was ten o'clock, and although the crowd was bigger than ever and the music kept pounding, most of the younger people like us were looking at watches and picking up sweaters and such. I tapped Katy's shoulder and pointed, and she told Jimmy, and a few minutes later, we were all four back in the car.

Except this time, Katy sat in the front with Jimmy, and Eddie sat in the back with me. I wedged the big woolen blanket mostly between us and squeezed back into my own corner of the seat. Eddie opened a slow, wide smile, leaned away into his own corner, and said only, "I'd go dancing with you anytime, Molly. You're all right!"

In the front seat, Katy sat in the middle of the bench, pressed against Jimmy, who drove with one hand on the wheel, the other over her shoulder. That had to end when the road began to climb back over the ridge, and we all saw a pair of deer scampering across right in front of the headlights. Jimmy slowed, putting both hands on the steering wheel and giving a low whistle.

"Guess there's more on the road than just us," he commented. We all agreed, and the edgy risk of coming so close to the big animals kept us awake and watchful for the rest of the trip.

As we rode the last mile into town, I could see only one or two lights on. The village slept.

"Let us off here," Katy urged Jimmy as we reached the center of the village, where the top of my own river road met the main street. "So we don't wake up our parents." I guessed they were awake anyhow, waiting for us, but I figured Katy didn't want to spoil the evening with a stiff ending around her father — or mine.

"Okey-dokey," Jimmy drawled. He rumpled Katy's hair and pulled her close to him for a minute, and I was relieved that he didn't try to kiss her.

Eddie opened the door for me, and nodded, smiling. "Remember what I said, Molly. I'd dance with you anytime. There's a lot of summer still in front of us."

I smiled politely, and said I'd see, and then ran down my road, while Katy scooted over toward the house entrance behind the store. And in a rumble of dust, the boys drove away.

As I reached my house, the dark grief swept over me again, and fear, for my mother. How could I have been dancing and laughing? Into the kitchen I tiptoed, and peered into the back bedroom. My grandmother had fallen asleep, propped up halfway in the armchair. A bundle of blankets on the bed hid my mother. I reached to gently pull them straight and discovered she wasn't there at all.

"Me-Mere!" I hissed. "Mama's out of bed somewhere!"

My grandmother woke instantly, and we ran from room to room and then up the stairs. Not here! I woke my father. "Mama's missing!"

The three of us raced into the gardens. "Stop!" my father said abruptly, and we did. He bent close to the ground, moved quickly to the gate, and then pointed down the road. "The river!"

We ran as if we were seeking a lost child, racing against catastrophe. In the half-moon light, we ran calling and searching. "Mama!" "Caroline!"

She stood by the river, on a flat rock, hands raised toward the moon. She swayed from side to side, and as we drew close I saw her eyes were closed. My father raised a hand to stop us. Quietly he walked toward her, voice pitched low as if to a little child. "Caroline, Caro, what are you doing out here? Come on back to the house, it's time to sleep."

My mother stopped swaying, but still her eyes were shut. She whispered, "I can't sleep. It hurts, Charles. It hurts where they took the baby. It never stops hurting."

I held my breath as my father stepped all the way up to her and reached to wrap an arm around her.

"I know, Caro, I know. You're still bleeding," he added gently. The long wet bloodstains rippled along the sides and down the center of her nightgown. She stood in a small puddle, and I grabbed at my grandmother, panicky. Would Mama die from so much bleeding?

Me-Mere shook off my hand and moved closer to my mother, ready to help my father carry her and to put pressure on the injured womb.

My mother was still speaking. "Not just there, Charles. My heart's torn, too. That was our son!" Her voice rose in a quavering wail, and she fell back against my father, sobbing.

I stood still. The thought shocked me: my parents wanted a son. After two daughters, they wanted a son. Was it so strange? No. But something in me sobbed with fresh pain. I wasn't enough for them, was I? They wanted a son, like anyone would.

Now my grandmother and my father between them carried my mother back up the hill to the house. "Run ahead and open the door," Me-Mere told me sharply.

I ran.

What had seemed for an evening to be a return to normal life, to being an American teenager at a dance, with friends, happy, vanished in the June moonlight. So while my mother got tucked into bed like a small child weeping, I walked around the kitchen like an old woman, wiping the table, putting water on to heat for tea, and admitting what kept coming more and more clear: by Monday, I would be doing the village wash on my own, as my grandmother nursed my mother and as my father labored at the dam. How could Papa make things right when life was so hard and dangerous? My freedom ended here, I thought. I might as well forget about any more dances. And even school.

I would have to be the grown-up now, until my mother healed. If she ever did.

Which was when, after such a long silence, Gratia suddenly spoke to me: "That's what you wanted, wasn't it? To turn into a grown woman and leave me behind. Go ahead, see how you like it. I hate you anyway!"

"I love you anyway, Gratia," I tried to say.

But I was sure she wasn't listening.

·�֎·

Day after day, basket of wash after basket of wash, June ground to a close. A heat wave struck on the Fourth of July. It made little difference to me, in the hot kitchen where water boiled endlessly and my grandmother slipped in and out like a ghost of herself, making different teas and soups. Sometimes, when my father was home on a Saturday afternoon or a Sunday morning, she'd walk in the woods to gather plants: cattail roots, birch bark, dandelions, touch-me-not, plantain. Her garden suffered from lack of tending, but the herbs still grew, and with fresh sage and comfrey she made poultices and more teas. My mother lingered in bed, and at night a knotted string across the bedroom door assured my grandmother there would be no wandering, even in dreams.

My muscles ached, especially across my shoulders, and my hands grew raw and rough, despite nightly creams and once a rosemary ointment my grandmother offered, but it made me sneeze too much. The neighbors, courteous and kind, understanding, continued to bring their wash — and, from week to week, hot dishes and fresh bread appeared with the arriving clothes and sheets. I protested, but Mrs. Wheeler and Mrs. Willson and the others brushed it away. "You're doing all you can do," they said. "This is our way to help."

For the first few weeks, Katy came by after work each day. She arrived with strawberries fresh and sun warmed, and sometimes with a handful of molasses cookies. I skimmed the cream from the milk that was delivered twice each week and made shortbread desserts. She told me who was working where, and she showed me the sweetheart ring when Jimmy gave it to her.

"Eddie still asks about you," she reminded me the day after the Fourth. She'd been to the parade in St. Johnsbury with Jimmy and some of the other kids from town.

I sighed. "He's a nice boy, I guess. But I don't

have the energy to go out. Tell him I'm sorry, would you? Besides, he'll find somebody else."

"Aren't you sweet on him at all?"

"Nope." I rubbed more skin cream into my sore hands. "I don't have time to be sweet on anyone."

"Not even Henry Laporte?" Katy guessed. "He brings things from the store for you, doesn't he?"

"He's just helped out some, being a neighbor like everyone else. He hasn't been around for the last week or two, anyway." I knew Henry meant more than just helping, but most evenings when he stopped by, I was too tired even to smile my thanks. He never pushed. I repeated to Katy, "There's too much to do. I just don't have time to be sweet on anyone."

"You'll change your mind when your mother's better," she predicted.

"Maybe."

Katy knew, as well as I did, that my mother wasn't getting better. The house almost tipped backward from the heavy sickness and sorrow in the back bedroom. At least my father went to move soil and rocks each day, so his own sadness lifted a little. But not my mother's.

Katy pulled the ribbons off her twin ponytails and asked to borrow a comb. "It's so darned hot at the farm," she complained. "My hair's always a

mess, too. One more week, though, and the strawberry season will be done."

"And then you'll be packing," I guessed. "And shopping too, won't you? For clothes, for Montpelier?"

"I guess." She eyed me speculatively. "They give
scholarships, you know. With your grades, you'd get
a scholarship for sure. Miss Webster told me so."

Miss Webster. Last spring's school days were a
lifetime away. I said, "I don't even think I'll be going
to school here in Waterford in the fall. Someone's got
to hold things together here."

"Or at the new house," Katy pointed out. "You're
moving at the end of August, aren't you? Molly, your
new house is right across from the school. I bet you
could still go to classes."

"I guess," I agreed without enthusiasm. Getting
up early to start the stove and the water for the day's
wash, going to school, and coming straight home to
move the clothes from the soapsuds to the rinse and
the wringer: that didn't sound like a very good day
to me. Neither did moving to the other house. Still,
with the water in the new lake rising, what choice
was there?

The conversation provoked a restlessness in me.
After Katy left, I looked in on Mama and gave
Me-Mere a fresh pot of tea. She had a second bed

247

made up now in the back room. Mama had stopped bleeding at last, but nightmares and sleepwalking followed. My grandmother pulled her bed across the doorway now, each evening.

"Me-Mere, I want to take a walk for half an hour," I told her in a soft voice. I didn't want my mother to hear. "Will you be all right without me?"

She nodded. "But tell your father to come sit in the kitchen in case I need him."

I did. My father stood slowly, gathered his newspaper from the front-room table, and moved to the kitchen table without comment. I set a plate of cookies within reach for him, tidied my hair, and slipped out into the almost dark evening.

Walking up the hill into the village seemed senseless; surely there'd be some people out enjoying the relative cool of the evening, and I didn't want to answer questions about my mother. I was too tired to talk.

So I turned downhill, toward the river.

It struck me, as I listened for the low swish of the summer waters between the banks, that Gratia hadn't come talking in a long time. Not since the night Mama ran out of the house. *Well,* I sighed, *that made life a little easier.* I didn't miss her — at least, not the voice I'd heard since she'd drowned. I stared at the river, puzzled more by the water than by Gratia's absence.

The water lapped the stones, much higher than midsummer water should be. I sat on the large flat rock at the foot of the river road and looked down, then across at the other bank. Definitely too high: almost as high as spring runoff, but not wild like spring water.

Oh. Dummy, I told myself. *It's rising. It's becoming a lake.*

Many of the familiar mid-river rocks were already hidden. *This won't be Fifteen Mile Falls anymore,* I reflected. The fragile sparkle of the nighttime lake only emphasized how dark and deep the waters under the surface were becoming.

At least, I noted, Gratia wasn't under the waters. Her little bones and the ones of my—our—baby brother lay together in the village cemetery. That was a good thing, wasn't it?

From behind me came the scuff of a shoe, as if someone had approached quietly, then thought to warn me. Without turning, I smiled faintly. Was it Henry?

It was. He sat quietly on another flat rock, and I nodded hello, then turned back to watching the river. I could just barely hear Henry's breath, along with the water sounds, and the chorus of small frogs, with an occasional gulp from a distant bullfrog. In the field on the other side of the river, fireflies flew, tiny green-yellow lights dancing over the open space.

"There were wolves here a hundred years ago," Henry commented at last.

I turned in surprise. "Why are you thinking about wolves?"

"Hmm. I wasn't exactly. I was thinking about change."

"Oh." The river made small lapping sounds at our feet. "Like the river becoming a lake?"

"Mmm. And farming. When the People of the Dawnland lived all along the river, they grew corn in the fields. Like this one, maybe."

I added to the sequence. "And then there were more deer, probably."

"And then more wolves to balance the deer herds. But when the English farmers came and raised sheep, they killed the wolves."

"And now the river," I mused. "The river becomes a lake."

Over the water, wings fluttered. At first I thought it was a late swallow, hunting for an evening meal. Then I noticed the twitch and leap of the flight, and I knew it was a bat. It fluttered above the water, making quick dips as it found mosquitoes or other insects.

I drew a deep breath. "Our house will be under the lake. At least, what's left of it. The crew will knock it down. We're moving at the end of the summer."

"More change. A hard one, probably." A matter-of-fact reply, with a hint of sympathy.

After a moment, I asked, "Were you away?"

"For a while. I'm here for the weekend, to help bring in the wood my father's cut. Then I'll go back to Lunenburg. Baskets."

I queried politely, "Have you made a lot of them this summer?"

"My mother and sister make them," he reminded me. "But I cut the ash and gather the willow, and they're working with sweetgrass this summer, too."

"I love the scent of sweetgrass baskets."

"I brought you one." From a pocket he pulled a small round basket with a lid. I couldn't see the weave in the darkness, but as he set it on my palm, it felt warm from being carried, and the warmth gave the grass more scent.

I lifted it and sniffed long and happily. "Thank you."

"You're welcome. I brought one for your mother, too." Another came from a different pocket.

My voice caught, and I cleared it. "She'll like that, I think." I teased a bit, "A third one for my grandmother?"

He smiled, shook his head no, and pointed to a wrapped bundle behind him. "Wintergreen. I thought maybe she could use some. Fresh from the woods today."

"Help me bring these all home," I invited. And he did—but refused to come in, saying he hadn't yet seen his father. He'd be back, he said.

What he left with me, besides the basket, was a sort of calm I hadn't felt in weeks. River or lake, house or home, change or not.

·�֎·

The rest of July was rain, rain, rain. And my father
came home from work at the dam in early August
and said, "We'll move next week. The lake's coming
up faster, and there's no sense getting into a race with
the water."

I nodded, barely looking up from the evening's
ironing. I wasn't surprised. Just worried. I knew I
could manage packing the house, as long as my father
took care of the heaviest furniture and his tools, and
I was sure he would. What I didn't know, though,
was how my mother could adapt to the move. Loss
after loss: the baby, her strength, and now our home.
Me-Mere, though, said it would be a good change.
With a fresh place and neighbors passing the windows

each day, my mother might start to take an interest. We planned to set the most comfortable chairs at the new front window, and we'd see whether it would work.

On Saturday the sixteenth of August, two men from the village arrived with a wagon and a pair of boys to help. Mrs. Wheeler and her niece came bright and early to help pack the last of the kitchen, and I expected Katy in the afternoon, when she and her mother came back from shopping in St. Johnsbury. We waited till the end to move the back bedroom, and my mother, snug in a blanket, for the afternoon was cool and a stiff breeze teased the leaves. Carried to the wagon and tucked into the corner of the front bench, she sat up and looked around her. A bit of color reached her cheeks.

Maybe Me-Mere is right, I thought. *This change may help.*

Seated in the rocking chair, in the new kitchen, my mother watched Mrs. Wheeler and Sara and me put dishes and pans into the cupboards. The scent of the room bothered me. Oh, it was clean, and part of what I could smell was soap flakes, and part of it was old house wood, waxed and polished. But there was also the presence of someone else, of old Mrs. Wells and people like her. I missed the undernotes of cedar and sage, cloves and cinnamon, even of laundry, that clung to our kitchen at home.

Grimly I corrected my thought: This *was* our home now. Better get used to it.

My grandmother, one eye on my mother and talking gently with her all the time, mixed together an herbal tea that provided some correction to the kitchen air. For my father and the other men I made coffee and sandwiches. The men ate quickly and went back to last-minute work at the dam site just past one o'clock, leaving us to cope with piles of blankets, boxes of dishes, sacks of clothing. I was glad that Sara and her aunt stayed on, putting things away as best they could and speaking now and then to my mother. Even though she never answered them, she smiled from time to time. The piles disappeared quickly, and when Katy arrived at three, she brought a white bakery box filled with powdered sugar donuts. So the first get-together in the new kitchen was a party.

Still, we all watched my mother closely, and soon Mrs. Wheeler and my grandmother helped her to the "new" back bedroom and into bed.

Katy and Sara moved closer at the table. "Well, tell us about the new clothes," I demanded. Katy beamed.

"The best part is, no more lace collars," she

declared. "And I've got a short jacket, of boiled wool, green with black buttons. I wanted red," she said with a wicked grin, "but my mother wouldn't let me. Anyway, green's a good color for an Irish gal, right, girls?"

We agreed. "And stockings?" Sara asked eagerly. "Did you get stockings?"

"Not yet," said Katy. "I can only get one pair, you know, they're so costly, and we're waiting until we're in Montpelier. My mother says the prices will be better there."

Sara added a long description of her own new outfit for school. She was going into tenth grade, and used to hand-me-downs from her cousins, so a brand-new store-bought skirt and blouse made big news for her.

I got up to fill the teapot another time with hot water, making the tea leaves do again for the refill. Everything that cost cash money needed to be stretched. The washing most often was paid for in trade now, eggs and maple syrup and garden vegetables, and even a ham from one family. My father's wages from the summer at the dam site would pay the taxes on the new house, but not much more than that. We were fortunate, I knew, that the power company had paid for our old home, a big part of what it cost to buy the other house, so we wouldn't have a mortgage.

Stretch it out, make it do, mend it, use it again. For a moment, envy rose in me: envy for Katy's new school and clothes, and for Sara's childlike enthusiasm. I wondered whether I'd ever feel excited again. A mound of wash had already arrived on the new porch, and I'd started heating water in the copper boiler — it steamed, and I paused to add soap flakes.

Back at the kitchen table, I hid my rough hands in my lap and tried to see the bright side. At least I had company, and a break from work, and so far, Mama seemed to be taking to the new house.

After the girls and Mrs. Wheeler left, though, I sank lower in my thoughts. What hope did I have? Bone tired, I dragged clothes out of baskets, grated more soap, and unloaded boxes of bottled preserves and applesauce into the lower cupboards in between. A knock at the side door turned out to be Miss Webster, with a dish of ham and beans for supper, and the kindness left me weepy and somehow more tired than ever.

A good night's sleep is what I need, I decided. Rashly, I postponed the next round of ironing and dedicated my evening to a hot bath and early bed. Even so, that meant trying to sleep in a new bedroom. I didn't have the energy to hang my own clothes, which lay in a mound on my unmade bed. So I moved them onto the top of the dresser and wearily tucked a sheet over the mattress. I wrapped myself in my own familiar comforter, its threadbare cotton smooth against my arms and legs, and I tucked one arm under my head—tomorrow I would find my pillow, which must have gone to some other room.

From the faint evening glow reflected on the white ceiling above me, the room held a little light. Everything I could see in that gray shimmer made me more tired: clothes to hang, the pier glass to fasten to the wall, a heap of winter clothing and blankets. I smelled the tickle-my-throat aroma of cedar and mothballs, as well as a summer evening damp and flowery, slipping across the room. My window opened toward the village; there was no sound of the river. Such an absence of the familiar must surely have kept me wakeful, yet exhaustion overwhelmed me and I slipped into sleep without even a moment of prayer.

Sunday morning brought more rain, so after carrying the winter blankets out of my bedroom to the chest in the hall, I spent the day struggling with, of course, more washing. I hung wet clothes to air on wooden racks in the kitchen, hoping they wouldn't go bad before the sunshine returned. Again I tried to take some of the day easier, and settled for scrambled eggs and biscuits for supper for us all, with thick slices of bacon on the side for my father. Monday, I knew, would mean more wash, more work. Resolutely, I set soup to simmer overnight on the back burner, tidied the kitchen, and pushed tables and chairs into fresh places until I thought it looked more homey.

Me-Mere wandered through, nodding, and said she was ready to do mending all evening. She retreated to the back room, and at one point I heard her singing, with my mother's voice, faint but fresh at last, joining in. My father came in from the woodshed and listened, and we smiled at each other through our weariness. Maybe Mama would come back to herself at last.

·✾·

But on Monday, everything fell apart. Everything.

It began with rain in the night—hard rain on the roof, rain and a violent strong wind more like November than the end of summer. Thunder crashed, and spears of jagged lightning whipped and crackled. I jerked awake, sitting up in familiar sheets but in an unfamiliar space. I waited for the next flash of lightning to show me the room, not wanting to stumble over bags and boxes. Wrapping a sweater over my nightgown, I padded quickly down the stairs. I heard voices in the back bedroom.

"The river! The river!" It was my mother calling out, my grandmother trying to hush her. "My baby's in the river! Gratia's in the river—somebody save her!"

My father crowded into the room with us all, in his work trousers without a belt, the thin cotton of a singlet over his chest, his shoulders bare. Me-Mere moved aside, letting him hold Mama. "I'm here, Caro, I'm here," he rumbled as he drew her firmly against his chest and rocked back and forth. "It's only a storm. Everyone's safe."

I marveled at how he'd gone right past my mother's words, to the fear in her. Gathered in against him, she stopped calling out. "Charles?" she murmured, in the tone of a sleepy child. "Charles, where's my own bed? I'm tired, Charles, I'm so tired."

"Hush," he said, "this is a good bed here. My mother's sharing her room with you tonight. It's a good safe bed."

Me-Mere whispered something, and my mother smiled. I slipped back out of the room. Half a step forward, half a step back, but they didn't need me in the room. I looked around the kitchen in the flashes of lightning, stirred the soup, added a small stick of wood to the stove, and climbed the stairs again. Running my hand along the unfamiliar railing, I resolved to clean more of the house in the morning, with our own cleaning things, so it would smell more like a real home to me.

I closed the wet bedroom window down to the

last half inch and sat on my bed to watch the storm. Torrents of rain fell. I could hear the pounding on our roof, and in the lightning flashes, I saw the dark school building across the road, the empty school yard, the muddy road between. Maybe it was raining too hard for people to bring much wash. I pictured a gentle Monday, one with time for settling, for cleaning, maybe even for reading a book. A Monday where I could feel like myself again.

A bell began clanging loudly, not from the church but from the firehouse. I knew what it meant: some barn, some house, something struck by lightning was aflame. In just a few minutes, men ran through the village toward the firehouse. I propped the window up a little wider and peered into the darkness, but I didn't recognize anyone in their raincoats and tramping boots. Then I heard trucks starting: the fire truck, the pumper, was headed out, and more trucks were following it.

I leaned out the window to see where they were going. And they were going—down the river road. Oh, no!

I flew down the stairs with one hand over my mouth, trying not to call out and frighten my mother. At the back bedroom door I gestured to my father, who read my face and surrendered his hold on my mother's curled-up form, with my grandmother smoothly taking over, crooning and singing and stroking my mother's hair.

Back in the kitchen, I told my father: "There's a fire. The lightning. Our house!"

He stared at me, a new despair in his gaze. I said, "I'll get your shirt and socks," and ran lightly up to his room, tugging loose a long-sleeved shirt from the nearest mound of clothes. Socks? There. I brought them down to him, and he scrambled into boots and jacket and cap and stumbled out the side door.

"God, keep him safe," I mumbled. For a moment I stood, unsure what to do next. Make tea? Pull on my own clothes and go down the street?

I'd be in the way. The men never wanted women or children at the fires, I knew. I surveyed the kitchen, wondering what we'd left behind at the old house for later moving. The third wash boiler, I knew; and oh, of course, the firewood, split and stacked in the shed. Things hanging in the porch. Spare boots, still huddled under a bench, and probably more of my father's tools for the woods. His snowshoes, and oh, no, my grandmother's garden baskets, all hand-made, all stacked for another day of picking up odds and ends.

Mechanically, I filled the kettle, set it on the

stove to heat, then stood at the porch door, seeing an orange and red glow down the hill and a yellow sickly color that hung in the sky even as the storm flashed and tore.

My childhood is burning, I thought. Which reminded me: I had left something of my own at the house to move later. My old diary. Now even the pages would vanish in smoke.

Hours later, in the sullen light of a stormy day, my father came home. His boots, his smoky jacket and cap, even his shirt, he left on the porch. I saw him look around at the neighboring houses with their possible views of our small screened-in porch, then step inside the kitchen to pull off his stained wet trousers before hurling them back out into the entryway.

I looked aside to give him some privacy and said, "Breakfast in five minutes," as he tramped up the stairs.

"Better make it ten," he replied. "And bring me some water to wash with."

I set a bucket of hot water outside his closed bedroom door, said, "It's out here," and went back down to the kitchen. In the promised ten minutes, he returned, dragging a chair out from the table and collapsing into it. I waited until coffee and eggs and three pieces of bread were inside him before I asked: "How bad?"

"Bad," he sighed. "The roof's gone of course, and the house is gutted. About all that's left is the porch, I guess."

I digested the news. "So maybe Me-Mere's baskets?"

He nodded. "I pulled them out. And the ax and saws. That's about it."

Sitting across the table with my own cup of coffee, I thought it over. I asked him: "The firewood?"

"Gone." He added with a hint of bitterness, "It burned nicely."

Me-Mere came out of the back bedroom, and I told her. She shook her head. "Maybe it's for the best," she finally said. "Two babies lost there. It was a sad place."

Nobody answered, although I think we all agreed.

Soon my father left, to help clean the firetruck before going to work. Though the men at the power plant site would all know about the fire, the dam boss would expect my father to be there as soon as he could.

·�֎·

As I stirred the copper boiler of wash, the children's song "Here We Go Round the Mulberry Bush" kept circling in my mind. "This is the way we wash the clothes, wash the clothes, wash the clothes, this is the way we wash the clothes, so early Monday morning." Except it was afternoon. And considering the steadily pouring rain, doubtless there'd be more wash tomorrow, arriving from farm families who hadn't sent their wagons out in the storm. In the song, Tuesday was ironing day, Wednesday mending, Thursday cleaning; this week, I saw, washing would stretch for two or three days, ironing for two more. Well, maybe my grandmother would be able to do some of the cleaning. If, that is, my mother calmed down.

She slept, childlike, in the back bedroom most of the day, worn out from the inner and outer storms of her night. Me-Mere drifted back and forth from kitchen to bedroom door, and sometimes up the stairs, to assess and start to claim the house. She stood at the windows, staring at the unfamiliar gardens. "Mostly grass," she sniffed. "And no berry bushes."

We agreed that probably the firefighters had trampled the gardens "back at home." Yet the weather showed few signs of letting up; she would have to wait until the next morning to go down the road and find out how much damage there was.

"All this rain is filling the lake too," I mentioned, and she nodded.

"Maybe the Long River will rest a bit longer in this place when there's a lake," she speculated. "Without the falls, it will be quiet." She paused, then continued, "Still, a free river has the best voice."

"Mmm." What good was a wild, free river's voice if the voices of the dead braided themselves into the song, I thought. For a moment I had a sense of Gratia, and I froze, waiting for her voice—but it passed. *Maybe she doesn't belong in this house,* I decided. It would be a relief. I had loved the angel sister, but there was no way I could change her death.

A growl of thunder in late afternoon worried me

that Mama would become upset again, but it faded without more fuss, and only the rain continued. The steady pounding on the roof and windows, the gray of the evening, and my father's arrival home, exhausted and unwilling to talk, all joined in a numbing that I welcomed. That night, in bed, I thought, *Tomorrow will be a new day.* Then I remembered I'd thought the same thing about today while yesterday was ending.

·❈·

Tuesday, however, dawned clear and fresh. Scrambling among a hodgepodge of clothes from the piles in my new bedroom, I resolved to place everything in the drawers and wardrobe before the end of the day.

But first things first, and first things, at six in the morning, were coffee and breakfast for my father and starting the wash water heating. My father's smoky clothes from Monday's fire would need a separate wash, I decided. Wash boilers, coffee, the stove itself—I sweated in the heat and propped open all the windows as well as the door out to the little "village-sized" porch. There'd be no room here for my grandmother's baskets, which sat in a soggy, smoky heap in the yard. I separated them, turning them upside down to dry in the morning sun. The outdoor air held a crispness like early September. Well, I estimated, if you called the start of school the beginning of autumn, the change of season was only a week or two away. I drew a deep breath and realized there were apple trees nearby—two large ones, close to the house. Me-Mere would like that.

Inside again, I stirred up pancakes for breakfast, and my father ate quickly, accepting the cold lunch I wrapped, and walked to the store to meet the truck full of men headed to the dam. Now the water was rising quickly, so that each day they tested, moved, repaired, cleared. Most of the crew members now were local men; the hundreds needed for the bulk of the construction had left, and their village of cabins and bunkhouses was slowly being taken apart for lumber for other projects in other places.

In the side yard, beyond the walkway for visitors, clotheslines stretched between two poles. While the water on the stove heated, I inspected the lines, finding them in good condition, if a little shorter than the ones I'd had at home. For now, they would have to do. Next spring, I could ask my father to make them longer. Thinking of season after season of doing wash almost stopped me, but there was no time for despair. Instead, I looked again at the sunshine filtering through the apple trees, and marched back into the kitchen to add an armful of clothes to their steaming, sudsy bath.

By noon, two loads of wash were on the lines and two more had arrived, as I'd expected. The surprise of the day came with my mother's condition: somehow the storm of the previous day had cleared her, rinsed her of some burden. She sat wrapped in a shawl, rocking next to the kitchen stove, occasionally making suggestions or comments about the clothes as I sorted them, colors and whites, for the next round of washing.

My grandmother asked whether I could spare her for a few minutes. I knew she wanted to check the gardens at our old house. "Go," I assured her. "Mama and I will have our noon dinner, and you can have yours when you come back."

When Me-Mere reappeared, she held a basket of vegetables and a handful of roadside flowers—daisies and Queen Anne's lace and red clover and purple bellflowers. She put them gently into Mama's lap before filling a jar with water to hold the blossoms. A small shake of her head warned me not to ask about our old house. I waited until Mama was napping in the back room.

"How bad?" I asked my grandmother.

"It's gone," she said simply.

I sat at the table and put my face in my hands. "I'm so tired," I admitted. "Tired of bad things happening."

I felt her hands on my shoulders, rubbing gently. After a bit, she said, "Go take a walk. I'll watch the wash, and your mother. She'll sleep for a few hours now."

So I set aside my apron and went outside into the changed world, the village yard, the afternoon sunlight. Across the way, Miss Webster, carrying a satchel of books into the schoolhouse, waved to me. *Oh*, I thought, *she must be making the classroom ready.* I waved back, but I didn't want to talk, so I gestured toward the store and she accepted the message — shopping to do.

Actually, what I wanted was to see the remains of our house. Rather than walk along the main street to the store, I turned down the river road. The smell of burned wood grew strong. I could see the blackened timbers above the trees, and the farther down the river road I walked, the more of the burned shell of the house stood revealed.

My chest tightened. When I reached the house, I walked in a circle around it. Wisps of smoke and steam still rose from some parts. Most of the burned wood had fallen into the cellar hole, although one wall, by the old kitchen door, still stood.

Around the other side of the house, I realized the river had come closer—or the lake, really. It lapped at the lower edge of the garden. How long would it take to reach the house itself? Maybe a week more, I guessed.

The smell of the burned house and its contents was dark and thick, something like a bonfire but heavier and bitter. Shards of window glass sparkled in the trampled yard. The chimney bricks spilled in a mound, dirty and wet. Trees close to the house were burned, their blackened sides damp and charred. My climbing tree was only half burned, but I didn't try to go up it in my good skirt, though I longed to step back in time.

I knew I should go back to the new house, to my grandmother and sleeping mother. For a moment longer I hesitated, looking at the battered gardens, wondering whether there was anything I should pick to bring back with me. No, I'd let Me-Mere sort that out.

I started up the hill. From this distance, the white gleam of the "new house" shone between the trees. Some of the leaves had already turned color. A cluster of vivid scarlet maple leaves caught my eye, dancing in a gust of wind. A new season.

AUTUMN

Living across the road from the school and not going to classes there: What could be stranger? I watched the children in line in the morning sometimes, but most days I was already working. Katy wasn't here anyway, which eased it a bit. If I'd had to watch Katy standing there, maybe talking with a new best friend, that would truly have hurt.

Instead, once a week Miss Webster brought a satchel of books and assignments, and I worked on them in the evenings. She insisted that if I completed them well, I'd still be able to earn a teaching certificate next year. I couldn't tell her that I'd never wanted one; it would hurt her feelings. Although I'd never gone to see her over the summer, she clearly believed

I would have gone, like Katy, to Montpelier's teachers college. Now I felt there was little choice: gain a teaching credential or wash other people's clothes for the rest of my life. I resolved to finish the books within a year and take the examinations in time to seize some position the following autumn.

With September's cool days and frosty nights, the leaves turned golden and red and deep brown, depending on whether they were poplars, maples, or oaks. In the yard at the new house, the apple trees bent low with fruit, and my grandmother and I took turns harvesting. Though the apples were wormy from lack of care, cut carefully they could become good applesauce and even pie filling for the winter.

I wondered when Henry and his family would come back from the summer grounds in Lunenburg. Sometimes I held the small sweetgrass basket he'd brought me in the summer and inhaled its fragrance of peace and sunshine. But I hadn't seen him in so long. Would he come to the house as soon as he returned? What could be keeping him?

One Sunday afternoon, with my father home to help Me-Mere with my mother, the three of them sitting over coffee at the kitchen table, I said I needed some air, and slipped out for time on my own.

I walked the road out of the village, past the turn

to the Laporte farm, sure that if Henry had come back, he would see me somehow, as he always did. No quiet "hey" came from behind me, though, even after I turned onto the rutted road through the golden woods toward the dam. I scuffed my feet to make the leaves fly up and crackle. A flock of geese, calling to each other, swung by overhead, aimed north. *Fool birds,* I thought, *fly south, south.*

A lot more trees had been cut near the dam site. The blue waters of the lake sparkled in the distance; the high stone walls blocked my view of the nearer part. I found a dry log and sat, looking at the man-made waters. No, just man-stopped; the waters were older than the people, that much I knew.

At last a deliberate slide of feet behind me suggested someone coming. I turned. Yes. He seemed taller, I thought, and deeply tanned, and he came and stood next to the log. I stood up also.

"Why were the geese flying north?" I asked right away.

"Feeding," he replied. "Headed for the last of the cornfields, no doubt. Wait a few more weeks, then they'll go south."

"So-o-o." I couldn't stop smiling. "When did you get back here?"

He ducked his head in apology. "About a week

ago, but I needed to help my father right away before I could take time to visit. Getting the last of the hay in, fixing the barn roof." With a wide gesture, he hinted at cows, gardens, a world of farm efforts. "If you hadn't come walking, I'd have called in the village this evening."

"You would?" A wild happiness caught my breath.

"Of course." He stepped closer and touched my hand with his. "I missed you. Even the woods aren't as sweet when you're not in them."

"Oh!"

Henry's hand moved to brush against my cheek. I stood still, except for the tremble that shook me. I could smell the woods in his clothes and the warm and somehow familiar scent of his skin. Mirroring his movement, I, too, lifted a hand and brushed my fingers against his cheek, stroking down along his jawline. His dark eyes held me, and I remembered when I'd sobbed against his chest after the baby's early birth and death. He said gently, "Let's sit together."

So we did, side by side, our legs warm against each other. He wrapped one arm over my shoulders, and I rested against the faint heartbeat that I could feel through the side of his chest.

After a while he asked, "Your mother?"

"A little better," I replied. "She sits in the kitchen now, in the mornings, even though she sleeps most of the rest of the time. And she's eating a little." Still terribly thin, but there was no need to tell everything at once. "I don't think she remembers much about the baby now. Mostly it's Gratia—my sister, who died in the river, when she was five years old—mostly it's Gratia she talks about." It was easier to hear my mother talk about Gratia than to listen to Gratia speak, in that bitter tone I used to hear. But I hadn't heard much of the voice of my older, little sister since the move into the new house, away from the river.

"And village life?"

I laughed. "I thought we lived in the village before, but I guess we were well outside of things. Now I hear every wagon and truck, people come calling, and the school is just across the road. Today's the first day I've tasted real quiet in weeks." I turned my face up toward his. "Your sister, your mother? The baskets?"

"A good summer," he confirmed. "And the baskets are already sold. Winter can come when it pleases; there's only a little more wood to cut."

Sparse though the words were, I heard satisfaction

and contentment under them, and nodded. My hair rustled against his woolen shirt, and he smoothed it away from my face. He fingered the long hair at the back of my head.

"No braid?"

"No." I pulled away a little to look into his face. "Not even a small one now. The newspapers still talk about the right kind of Vermonters." Braided hair always held meaning for the People of the Dawnland. But my grandmother and I held to our decision to "brush it out and make it look pretty" for now.

Henry nodded. I felt him twisting a bit of my hair into the start of a braid, then fingering it back to smoothness. He met my gaze and asked directly, "Do you miss it? Being Indian on the outside?"

"More than I thought I would," I confirmed. "I guess I'm trading it, though, for the inside." We shared a smile, understanding each other.

I added, intently watching for his reaction, "My grandmother thinks the nurses who came when my mother — when the baby came too soon — she thinks the nurses did something to my mother to stop her from having more babies."

Pain creased the soft skin around his eyes. "She could be right. Other people at the summer fields were talking about doctors who cut, and the governor wants his new law."

"What will we do?"

To my anxious question, first, Henry drew me back closely against him, letting the security and warmth give one kind of answer. Then he said, "Keep each other safe."

I thought about keeping my family safe, too, and wondered about his. I wanted to meet them now. And I remembered the way my aunts and uncles had come to us when the baby died. With the cold season deepening, it was time to invite them again. I would remind Me-Mere.

Then Henry added softly, "And we'll wait a bit."

"Wait a bit for what?"

"To have babies," he said into the top of my head, laying a single soft kiss there.

The words and their meaning silenced me. I pressed more tightly against him, moving one of my arms to wrap around his waist. We sat in the sunshine, saying nothing more, for quite a while.

When the cool air began to settle around us, it was time to go. In fact, I realized I'd been away much longer than I meant to be. I told Henry, and he said, "I'll walk you home. It would be good to say hello to your family, anyway."

"Good," I agreed. We walked slowly back up the woods road, holding hands, but when we came close to the village, we let go. It didn't matter—the closeness was there, no matter what anyone else could see. I drifted in a sun-warm lake of contentment.

For me, the working week began in an unusual daze of happiness. Henry's visit to my family, a short but warm one, pleased everyone. My grandmother sang happier songs to my mother afterward, and my father told me that night, "He's a good man. I'm glad you brought him home." Of course, none of them knew how much Henry and I felt about each other, what we had said in our time out by the dam Sunday afternoon—but there was no hurry to tell more. And meanwhile, the important part was, I liked myself and my life when Henry was in it. So I had no doubts.

Only one dark shadow fell into the week, and it happened Tuesday morning at breakfast, when my father looked up from his oatmeal and coffee and said, "Tomorrow the bulldozers are coming." To my puzzled look he added, "They'll bulldoze what's left of the house. Push it into the foundation, so the waters move over it smoothly."

Oh. Why hadn't I thought about that? I knew that some other buildings farther upriver had been knocked down when they stood within the borders of where the new lake would be.

"How close are the waters, then?" I asked.

"Spilling into the cellar," he said grimly. "We'll only be able to push from the other side, and it'll still be dangerous. Someone forgot to schedule it sooner."

After he'd left, I whispered the news to my grandmother, who said she'd need to go to the old garden to dig up a few more roots. It would have to be today. We agreed, and it seemed a good day for my mother. We settled her into her rocking chair and gave her some mending to hold, perhaps even stitch. Though she still spoke little, I thought Mama was coming alive again in the new house. For this, despite everything, I was glad we had moved.

At midmorning, my mother suddenly said, "I want to get your father's blue shirt. It needs a new button. I want to go upstairs."

I said I'd run for it in a moment, but she said,

"No, I want to go up there myself." And she carefully stood, smoothed her skirt, and moved toward the stairs.

Amazed, I followed, and kept right behind her as she climbed the steps, one at a time. At the top, she sat for a few minutes on the blanket chest, catching her breath, coughing a bit. She asked me to fetch a spoonful of honey.

"Yes, but don't move while I do," I told her firmly, and I ran down to the kitchen. When I returned with the spoonful of honey, held carefully over a small bowl, I was relieved to find her still sitting quietly. She took the honey, and the cough eased.

Because I was so close to her, I felt the confusion in her thinking as she looked around at the three doorways, unsure which to choose. I guided her to the first, the room where my father slept. For a moment I saw it through her eyes: piles of clothes, folded and clean but not shelved, sat on the dresser. A pillow and tossed blanket showed he'd slept there—but only in half the bed. The other half waited for her, as if she'd only been gone from it a few hours instead of months. She drew a long thin breath and whispered, "I need to sleep here with your father."

"Yes, I know," I answered, thinking about what it meant to want to be close to someone all night. It distracted me a moment, and I suddenly realized my mother was climbing into the bed, clothes and all, pressing her face to the pillow where my father had slept.

"Mama, let's go back downstairs," I said gently. "If you want to sleep up here tonight, Papa can help you then."

"Have to rest now," she murmured into the pillow. And in that instant, she fell deeply asleep, arm curled around the pillow, cheek snug against what I knew must be the scent of the man she'd loved so long. I couldn't force myself to wake her and insist that she come right down again. But I had clothes to iron.

So I closed the bedroom door and propped an empty basket against it, planning that if she got up and opened the door, I'd hear the basket fall. And down the stairs I went, already concerned about getting the irons hot enough and whether the sheets were the right dampness to be pressed.

Just past noon, Me-Mere reappeared, heavily laden with a pair of baskets of roots and bulbs. She looked exhausted, gray faced. I pressed her to sit and urged her to eat, first soup, then bread, and sweet tea. Slowly the color came back to her.

"I haven't worked in the garden since your

mother—since the baby came too soon," she explained, head tilted like an inquiring bird to see whether I would believe her explanation. "That's all it is, I'm just not used to working."

"Mmm." I thought that was just a small part. Seeing the charred remnants of the house, the trampled gardens, must have been hard, and of course the house was where she'd given birth to her own sons. What had turned into a good change for me was far more of a loss for her this time. I rubbed her shoulders and said, "Don't worry."

"I'll just go check on your mother, then." She stood and headed for the back bedroom.

I stopped her and explained. Interest flickered in her eyes. "So," she mused, "your mother is coming awake again at last. Good." She settled into the rocking chair. "Then I'll sit here and mend a few things, and wait for her. Tell me again about the door and the basket."

I explained again, and she nodded. I brought her a sheet in need of darning in several places, one from a farm family, and she drew out needle and linen thread and began laying a neat grid of threads into the first of the holes. We worked companionably until about two thirty, when I laid the irons aside and folded the last pillowcase.

"Me-Mere? Can I leave you here to listen for a few minutes while I go to the store for sugar? We're almost out, and I want to start a cake for supper."

"Go," she said, waving from her seat, "go, and take some time to visit, too, if you like. Your mother won't wake up for hours yet. Go ahead."

"Well, I won't be hours." I laughed. "Baking takes time, and I've got work to do. I'll be right back." I pulled on a coat and drew a woolly toque over my hair. It was late September but felt colder, and there had been frost in some fields. The farmers already were predicting we'd have an early first snow.

At O'Connor's Store, several people shopped and Mrs. O'Connor made a fuss over me, pulling out a chair and saying, "I just had a letter from Katy — let me show you." So as she weighed and bagged two pounds of sugar for me, I read Katy's letter to her mother. It was all fresh news to me; since starting school in Montpelier, Katy had sent me one letter, the first week, homesick and doubting herself. Now, in her letter to her mother, I saw she'd gotten past all that. She wrote about new friends and a study group, and I missed her awfully as I read.

"Oh, don't go yet, dear," Mrs. O'Connor said when I stood up. "I wanted to show you the new mercerized thread we just got; I know you mend so much." So I spent another ten minutes with her and agreed to try the new thread, or rather to have Me-Mere try it.

"It does look as though it will thread into the needles better," I admitted.

"There, didn't I tell you? I knew you'd like it!"

I promised to report back to her, and paused another couple of minutes to say hello to the Reverend Witherspoon and a new couple coming to stay on one of the farms for the winter. Two children lingered by the candy jars, coins clutched in small hands. I realized I had entirely grown up, in comparison.

At last I headed for home.

Crisp leaves rustled underfoot. Scudding clouds propelled by cold winds interrupted the sun, but when the beams broke through, they lit the half-bare tree limbs like an illuminated picture. For a moment, in the sky, the sun splintered into a burst of rays over the western hills, biblical and glorious.

Our house was the next one, and I slowed, reluctant to go inside. I leaned on the porch railing, stretching out my shoulders, realizing it must be well after three, for the school yard stood empty, the windows dark. Bending, I picked up the cap to an acorn, thinking I'd blow against it like a whistle, the way children do — when, inside the house, I heard a scream and a series of heavy thuds, and I ran in through the kitchen door to find my grandmother startled out of a nap in the rocker and an unholy wail echoing from the foot of the stairs, suddenly turned to a shout of "No!"

Dodging around Me-Mere, I swung around the corner of the hall and saw, in a confused mound on the floor at the foot of the steps, my mother and another woman, dressed in white, both lying on the rag rug, the front door of the house partway open beyond them. With a quick shove, I closed the door. It was my mother who'd wailed and who was shouting "No!" over and over again as she beat against the white form.

I rolled the woman in white off my mother's frail limbs and tried to catch the flailing arms. "Mama! Mama, what happened?"

"She wants to kill my baby," my mother gasped, suddenly out of energy to yell. "She wants to kill my baby again. No! No!" She kicked desperately against the other woman's chest, then collapsed in a heap against me, eyes shut, speechless.

"Me-Mere! Help me!"

With my grandmother lifting her feet, I carried my mother to the back bedroom. Her pulse raced, her chest flicked up and down, and otherwise she was motionless. I told Me-Mere the words I'd heard. My grandmother clicked her tongue and tucked a blanket over my mother's fragile form. We stared at each other. What should we do?

"I'd better go see to the nurse," I said at last. "Maybe they fell down the stairs together. I don't know how much she's hurt."

But the nurse, I found, was not just hurt: The angle of her head, like that of one bloodied arm, was wrong. Whatever had taken place on the stairs, the nurse had the worst of it. For she was, unquestionably, dead of a broken neck. A puddle of urine had formed at her hips, and I smelled the sour hot scent of it.

Dear God, now what was I to do? I bolted the front door, wondering how it had been left unlocked for this stranger to enter, and I leaned against the wall, sickened by the death and by fear. What would happen to my mother once people knew a nurse had fallen and died in our house? What would happen to us all?

Panicked, I stretched past the woman on the floor—I could not call it a body, it was a person—and raced up the stairs to get the blanket from my bed. Unfolding the blanket over the woman lying there, I stopped and stared into the blank face. Could it be? Yes, I was certain. It was the older nurse, Nurse

Carpenter, the one who had pushed a blade between my mother's legs. My mother's terror made complete sense.

But had she pushed the nurse down the stairs? Or struggled with her at the top, so they both had fallen? Replaying the sounds I'd heard from the porch, that was most likely. I knew enough about the law to know my mother would never be called a murderer. Impatiently, I brushed the thought aside. What I needed now wasn't guilt or innocence or reputations. I needed a plan. What could I do?

I laid the blanket carefully over Nurse Carpenter. In an impulse I couldn't explain, I took the name-plate from her uniform and slipped it into my pocket. Then I stared at the mound on the floor, unable to decide on the next step.

Boots and voices sounded at the kitchen door. I leapt to my feet and met them in the kitchen: Henry and my father, both worried. Henry was saying, "I was up in the field, but I know I saw her run into the house like something was wrong."

My father called out, "Molly! There you are. Is something wrong? Is your mother all right?"

Out of the back bedroom came my grandmother, angry and hissing. "Quiet! Quiet! Take off those

294

boots, you know better! And sit down at the table, right now. When there's quiet here, we can talk."

I sat and leaned my head into my hands, which smelled of urine and sweat, so I stood again to wash them while the men took off their boots, chastened enough to hush their voices. "Is Caroline all right?" my father demanded.

"No!" Me-Mere threw the word at him. "But sit down! You can't do anything until you know what's happened."

"That's what I'm trying to find out!" My father pounded a fist against his leg, a gesture that clearly hurt more than it helped. I sat, and Henry pulled up a chair next to mine and brushed a hand against my arm.

When we all had seats, my fierce grandmother ordered me, "Tell them."

So I did.

A stunned silence hung over the table. I waited for my father to speak. He closed his eyes for a long moment.

"It was too late for another baby," he mourned. "It was too hard for her. It's my fault."

"Hmmph." My grandmother snorted. "She's still as likely as anyone to recover. Give her time.

Remember, she climbed the stairs today." She tapped impatiently on the table. "I'll tell you this: That Nurse Carpenter was a bad, bad person. At the least, she cut Caro to the point of terrible illness. And we'll never know whether she smothered that baby, either."

I jerked my gaze up at Me-Mere. The idea hadn't occurred to me. I just thought the baby had been born dead. Had the nurse made sure he didn't breathe? Shock made me cold, and I shivered. I felt Henry's warm hand cover mine on the table, in full view of the others.

The idea wasn't a new one to my father, it was clear. Clenching his teeth, he pounded a fist against his leg again.

Next to me, Henry cleared his throat. "If you don't mind, sir, I might have something of a plan."

"Spit it out," urged my father.

"Well, sir, assuming we don't feel obliged to report Mrs. Ballou's involvement in the death"—"darn straight we don't," muttered my father —"it seems to me that a person walking around the village might fall almost anywhere. But there's one place where, if she fell, she'd be sure to break her neck, sir."

We all waited. My father squinted at Henry appraisingly. "The dam, hmm? Good thought." He looked around the table. "If this young man and

296

I can move the woman's body to the dam, are we agreed that will be an end to this?"

Everyone nodded. Me-Mere rose to make tea and to try to get my mother to drink some. My father went to tie the blanket snugly around the nurse and move the wrapped body to the porch, where he set some lumber over it. I fetched a cloth for cleaning the hallway. Henry vanished down the road to borrow his father's farm truck. Reaching into my pocket for my handkerchief, I discovered the nurse's nameplate and handed it to my father. He looked thoughtful and tucked it into his shirt pocket.

And as the early autumn darkness closed in around the village, we moved a stack of lumber, and a soft blanket-wrapped bundle under it, to the bed of the battered blue truck. My father and Henry drove off, and Me-Mere and I finished cleaning and started thick beef soup and biscuits for supper. We took turns checking in the back bedroom, but my mother slept onward, her deep regular breathing both reassuring and disturbing.

"When do you think she'll wake up?" I asked my grandmother.

"When her mind is sure she was only having a bad dream," Me-Mere guessed. "And that's what we'll tell her if she ever asks."

And so it was agreed, and something of the darkness of the evening lifted in my heart, because we
were doing this for my mother — my mother who'd
been hurt in so many ways, and hadn't deserved any
of it.

In early November, an inspection team from the state, examining the spillway of the big new dam below the new lake, discovered a body in the rubble at the base of the wide stone and concrete wing, just beyond the area where the quieted river flowed out of the power company's penstock. The papers printed the news, and the village wondered who it could be, with people proposing names of various vanished cousins and ne'er-do-wells. Two days later, investigators found the nurse's nameplate in a crevice at the top of the wall, where they said it must have caught as she tumbled to her death. The power company installed a six-foot-high fence along the area and posted warning signs. I thought about the nurse's body going home to someplace else, with a proper burial; her spirit would not speak from the river.

My mother did not wake again to face this last terrible death. In a slow and gentle way, she faded day by day, until one morning we found her breath gone, her heart quiet. My grandmother had whispered safety and comfort to her daily for the autumn months, and she seemed to pass without pain, letting go of the lost babies, the shredded womb, the sorrows and pain. My aunts helped to sing over her at the end, and we laid her to rest next to Gratia and the baby. For me, this passing felt like the separation between a tree and its leaves in autumn, when a boundary forms between the source of nutrients and the blushing leaf. Then one day a whisper of wind takes it away.

Although my father seemed lost, my grandmother tended him, and he found work on the grounds of the power station. The job promised to become year-round work, at a good wage. He missed the adventure of the logs and the river. But the dam had ended any passage of logs down the Connecticut. My father wasn't the only woodsman grieving that change, and few realized he had deeper sorrows as well. Fear, too, although that was easing. No challenge came to the coroner's finding of accidental death for the dead woman found by the dam. Also, the state legislature held off action on the governor's demand for sterilization of the strangers among us, the different, the weak, the "unfit" among the plain New England family trees. Far too many state senators and representatives had found their own cousins in the scientific studies the university had sponsored, studies meant to pick out those unfit to be true Vermonters.

Late in November, Henry and I walked along the edge of the lake — *K'tchi Kwis'pam,* Henry called it, the large lake. In the village, they'd named it after the dam instead, Moore Dam Lake. To me, it was still the Long River, just with a big quiet belly of water. But I realized I might be alone in that vision.

The day was fiercely cold, already well below zero. As we stood where the river road once had led to my family's old house, we noticed an edge of ice along the rocky shore. *"Mzatanos,"* Henry murmured. "Freezing river." He was teaching me more words, and some of the old ways. My grandmother's offer of lessons in the woods next summer sounded good to me, too. I needed to know more of where and why my family had come here, especially when someday I might want to teach those things to children. If

I could teach things that were important — not just reading and arithmetic — maybe teaching wouldn't be so bad.

"Mmm." I took his hand and slipped it into my coat pocket with my own mittened hand, feeding the warmth between us. "I wonder."

He turned to look into my face and lifted his other hand to brush the hair back from my eyes. After a moment, he asked, "What do you wonder?"

"I wonder what secrets lie under the water now. What parts of other lives could be there? Some of the old logging men, I'm sure, with maybe even a horse or two. And the secret of why my sister Gratia slipped into the river that day. And — and other questions and answers," I finished softly.

Henry nodded. "It was a lighter place when it was still an open river, at least when summer came and the waters grew low," he mused. "Deep waters are darker. Soon the ice will close and make them darker still."

"Let's not live close to a lake, then," I suggested. "Let's live on an open hillside, with a brook, and nests of swallows, and a field where the geese will stop to feed."

"Mmm. A farm, maybe, with summer grounds cleared from the forest?" He was smiling. So was I.

"Close enough to visit Me-Mere and my father, though," I added.

"And for them to visit us."

The moon was rising. With each moment, the night grew colder, and as we watched, a fine tracery of lines formed on the still surface of the lake. The ice was setting in, closing the water for the winter.

"*Olegwasi,*" Henry whispered into the moonlight. "Good dreams, sleep well."

"Sleep well," I echoed. "Good night. I'll see you in the morning."

We walked up to the main street of the village, and I paused at the path to my father's house. Light as a snowflake, Henry set a kiss on my cheek, and I brushed my lips across his.

"Five months to April," he reminded me. "Five months until you'll be able to start teaching. A teacher and a farmer could do well to stay together. Become a family."

I nodded, not surprised. There was no need for speeches or fancy rings between us. We joined hands gently, promising each other a way forward from the dark and cold of winter, and a way through it, together. Surrounded by the small lights of the village, we did nothing more, and said no more.

I stood to watch Henry walk toward the farm,

until finally the cold drove me into the kitchen, the kitchen that Me-Mere and I would share until spring, when I would leave. Next April, I thought. At last, something to like about that month. I would have to write to Katy, to tell her.

Olegwasi.

Horrible though it is to think about, many American states in the 1920s and 1930s considered whether "unfit" people should stop having children. The ideas came directly from the way people understood the new discoveries in science. If you could breed better cows that gave more milk, why wouldn't you want people to think about having smarter babies? Americans wanted to be the best people in the world. For a while, changing the decisions around babies looked like a way to help Americans become smarter, stronger, even harder working.

In Europe, this idea became part of a nightmare of genocide (killing groups of people seen as somehow related: in Germany, that was the Jews, as well as Catholics and Gypsies and homosexuals). We know about it because we see pictures of the concentration camps and death camps of World War II. Ideas about killing or sterilizing unwanted people keep coming back in groups all over the world, though — in Africa, in Asia, in South America.

I love Vermont. My family has roots in Vermont, and although I grew up in "the flatlands" of New Jersey, I moved to Vermont as soon as I started having my own children. It's a good place to grow up, I think. So when I learned that Vermont had its own Eugenics Project — to clean up the people who lived in Vermont and make them stronger, smarter, better — I was shocked. Nancy Gallagher's book *Breeding Better Vermonters* told me a lot about the people, the ideas, and the actions in Vermont in the 1920s and 1930s around "eugenics," including the threat of sterilization of people who were too "different" from what Real Vermonters might be. For people with Abenaki heritage, these were nightmare years. In fact, if you look at U.S. Census numbers for "Native Americans" in Vermont, it seems as though all the Abenaki people disappeared at once! The numbers come back after 1970, when people felt it was safe to answer the Census questions honestly. Recently Vermont gave state recognition to the Abenaki people. However, their "disappearance" for so many years has prevented the federal government from recognizing the tribe.

Now you know some of the history behind Molly's story. You can read Nancy Gallagher's book, or investigate more through other resources that link to this book.

Every novel has roots in actual feelings and stories, or histories. Molly and her family are fictional. But there are real children and grandchildren here of Abenakis who lived through Vermont's frightening years and who now feel safe as they share stories of those days and people. I am glad they let me listen and read. The town of Waterford is real too; I live on a back road in Waterford, about five miles from where Molly Ballou would have lived. I've changed some roads and buildings, and I've simplified Waterford's two dams — and two historic changes in the Connecticut River — into just one for this story.

In Waterford today there are many good people who stand up for what they believe is right. I don't have any records of Abenaki families in Waterford (although there are plenty of records of them in the surrounding towns), but I think the people I know here would have helped Molly to keep her family safe.

·✳·

For reading, thinking, suggesting, and caring, I thank:
Gordon, Lois, Alexis, Lore, Katherine, Josette, Joe,
Nancy, Amy, Reeve, Robin, Kiril, Milan, and Julius;
my husband, Dave; wise and insightful editor Hilary
Breed Van Dusen; and George Nicholson, who saw
what it was all about.